Eamonn Mc Grath was born into a farming community in County Wexford in 1929 and he graduated in English literature at University College Galway in 1952. His first novel *Honour Thy Father* was originally published by Allen Figgis in 1970 and reissued by Blackstaff Press in 1990. *The Charnel House* is his second novel. Eamonn Mc Grath currently lives in Clonakilty, County Cork, where he is a teacher.

The
Charnel House

Eamonn McGrath

THE
BLACKSTAFF
PRESS

BELFAST

With grateful thanks to Dr Noel Browne,
Minister for Health in the first inter-party government (1948–51),
without whose enlightened policies this book
– and so much more –
would not have been possible.

04654464

CLITHEROE

3/91

First published in 1990 by
The Blackstaff Press Limited
3 Galway Park, Dundonald, Belfast BT16 0AN, Northern Ireland
with the assistance of
The Arts Council of Northern Ireland

© Eamonn Mc Grath, 1990
All rights reserved

Typeset by Textflow Services Limited
Printed by The Guernsey Press Company Limited

British Library Cataloguing in Publication Data
Mc Grath, Eamonn 1929–
The charnel house.
I. Title
823.914
ISBN 0-85640-447-0

for the few who survived,
and
in memory of the many who did not

'... it seems to me that a man needs to be unhappy
or poor or sick
– otherwise he'll become arrogant.'

from *On the Eve* by Ivan Turgenev

Thickening twilight as the night nurse came stealing. A soft hoot
of owls out over the dim fields, swooning in sleep towards the
misted river. Quiet fall of feet and the crisp whisper of starched
cotton. A brightness, a presence, a medicated essence, hovering,
retreating. Hiss of hinges. A rush of air and the unheard surge of
silence.

He lay there, dying as the evening died, but not gracefully
– without resignation. Outside, the sweet embalmed body of
a summer night. Inside, a foul human body, consumed by
a rage of bacilli. He smelt in disgust his damp hands, cursing
his mortality – unfinished hands, inexperienced hands that
would never love a woman, hold a child of his own, rancid
hands, already smelling of worms and winding sheets and
decay.

A bird falls from the air. An apple drops into the summer
grass. A snail is trampled into the roadway by careless feet.
Nature is prodigal, caring nothing for the individual life.

He had been taken up in a lift and bedded briskly in an airy ward
with four beds, two of which were unoccupied. In the other sat
a hunched figure, propped by pillows, his fevered skin stretched

1

over famined face, struggling to light a pipe – and coughing, coughing, coughing.

'Here long?'

'A year.'

A year!

'Going home soon?'

'Yes, soon.'

The following morning they had removed him hurriedly and at noon he heard that the man was dead.

People came to talk. Middle-aged schoolmaster – thick-rimmed glasses, sparse hair brushed back, exhausted air, and tired, cynical eyes.

'What kind of place is it? I'll tell you what kind of place it is. Did you ever read Dante's *Inferno*? I'd make it required reading for anyone coming in here. That inscription Dante saw over the gates of hell – it should be put over the front door.'

'What inscription?'

'*Lasciate ogni speranza voi ch'entrate.*'

'Meaning?'

'Abandon hope all ye who enter here.'

Another visitor. Gaunt, wasted frame, protruding scapulae like stunted wings, as he bent to sit. Hollowed cheeks, stretched skin – pale except for the dry flame on the cheekbones.

'Three months? They told you you'd be out in three months?' Short, breathless cackle. Rattle of phlegm in the scraggy throat as he turned aside to spit into a dark blue, screw-topped sputum bottle. 'Three months! You'll be lucky. That's what they tell everybody. Softens the blow, you see.'

Softens the blow! At nineteen, three months seemed a lifetime.

'How long have you been here?'

'Ten months. Last time it was eighteen, and the time before that ...' His voice tailed away.

'You were here before?'

'Maybe six years in all – out of the past ten.'

Silent plucking at the blankets, wishing him to go away, to leave the unspeakable unsaid.

'I'm what they call a chronic.'

'Oh …'

'We're all chronics. It's a death sentence.' The tired eyes looked at him, sizing him up, trying to infect him with their own deadly bacillus of despair.

A raging scream inside his head. Three months. I'm only here for three months. I'm different from the rest of you. I'm not going to die.

They were obsessed with death.

'Three funerals I saw leaving this floor in the one day.'

'In June, Stevie died.'

'A fine day it was. They were making hay down there by the river.'

'And Dick. You remember Dick from Bree?'

'Dick? Aye – pushing the daisies.'

'And McNally and Donoghue, and Jem Kehoe that had all the ribs out.'

'All dead, boy. All dead.'

It was an airy day in late April when he had first come to Ardeevan, a day of racing shadows and sudden gleams. The road from town unwound pleasantly along the floor of the valley. Tall beeches and sycamores overhead – brown tunnels and long vistas with green light filtering through. Between the boles there were glimpses of marsh-meadow on the right, slender reeds and the serpentining river. The land to the left rose precipitously, clothed in dense stands of timber and broken occasionally by hanging fields of gorse and by the gouged gash

3

of a limestone quarry. After a few miles, the high stone walls of an estate, a gate-lodge of burned brick, clinging like a barnacle to the keel of the hill, piers and a hairpin avenue. Massive open iron gates, soldered by rust into unclosable rigidity. At the top the avenue opened out into green lawns, bounded on one side by laurel hedges and trees, and on the other by fenced grazing land.

The sanatorium, a long three-storeyed building in raw brick – unmellowed as yet by time – stood, all glass and glitter, in the sunshine. Verandahs, with glass doors opening on to them, ran the length of the building. Inside, clinical steel beds were visible. Here and there along the verandahs patients in buff dressing gowns stood leaning across the railings. There was a fresh wind blowing, which gave the odd effect of coming suddenly round a bend and discovering a ship – its passengers airing themselves on deck – sailing through seas of grass.

Behind, at right angles to the new building and connected to it by a narrow stem, was the original house, once the home of Miss Grace, the last of the Challoner family, before she sold out and moved to Malahide. A Victorian Gothic curiosity, it had the same burnt and weathered brick as the gate-lodge, all gables and turrets and projecting balconies with balustrades of carved stonework, its roofs intricately valleyed, varying in pitch and height, the whole topped, as in some crazed mason's nightmare, by an extravagance of chimneypots. In front of the old house there was a gracious space, more weathered balustrading and a terraced descent to walks and walled gardens where ancient espaliered pear trees, gnarled and arthritic, still clung and drew heat into their barren fibres. Well to the back there was a walled yard, under whose cobbled archway in times past landed centaurs had ducked their

4

heads on their way to the stables after a hard day in the hunting field.

He lay in a little room off the corridor, his mind cut adrift, floating on clouds of vagueness, his sense of time and the sequence of events dulled and blunted. The door had been left permanently open and he was aware of people – official people, like nurses and doctors – coming to look at him. He was conscious of footsteps, voices on the corridor, words filtering in like the whispered sigh of wind – words that seemed to have some relevance to himself, syllables that struggled to coalesce into the shape of his own name, then broke up and floated away before he could refine his hearing and tune it in to their distant pulsing. He tried to concentrate, to alert himself to their coming, to lie in wait for them, to anticipate their arrival. But, inevitably, his attention would lapse and they would come again, faint and distant, like the signals from a receding galaxy. He felt that if only he could hear them, he would learn some secret about himself.

Once, he remembered coming out of darkness to find his mouth spouting a pink effervescent froth that came and would not stop, but gushed and bubbled like obscene champagne from an inexhaustible source. He had just enough energy to press the bell and hang drooling over his sputum mug until help came.

Swiftly they had put him lying flat with a pillow under his shoulders and his head tilted back. He was given an injection of morphine. Then a hot fomentation was placed on his abdomen and he was given ice cubes to suck until the flow stopped, and he lay there, pale and exhausted with a fine moisture on his forehead and the hovering faces blurring and floating indistinctly above him.

He knew he had received the last sacrament. He remembered the comforting whisper of the priest, the healing balm of oil

5

on eyes, ears, nostrils, mouth, hands and feet – though all he could clearly remember was his mouth and feet. He remembered the dry touch of cotton wool to his lips and the change in temperature as his feet were bared. The priest's hands were gentle and the whole ritual soothing as the drift of grace.

Voices again. It might have been his mother's voice he heard – anguished with the pain of birth and love and loss. But he couldn't be sure. Why was she so remote? Crows too – scraping on his consciousness, rasping through drowned memories, tearing in hoarse tumult down into submerged layers of himself, a quintessential self, fashioned of country sounds and enigmatic skies, of blustering winds and earth smells and green sap, rooted in the warm womb. Crows hieratic in the spring beeches, celebrating the sacramental crossing of twigs. The thin bleat of new life cradled on the high wind. Satisfaction and a sense of benediction that, in their wisdom, they had chosen his trees, his house.

In the evenings, his temperature rose, and after the night sweats, he shivered until they came and changed his clinging pyjamas and sodden sheets. Afterwards he lay there in the silence, his breathing troubled, while his mortality closed in on him like the mysterious darkness, and the faint spark that was he flickered and wavered, then, like a lamp turned low, steadied and held constant to light him through the shadowy labyrinths of sleep.

1

Sister Cooney sat in her office at the head of the corridor, a pile of manila folders in front of her. She removed one from the bundle, opened it and made an entry with a fountain pen, examined it carefully to see if it was dry, then laid a sheet of blotting paper on it and drew her clenched fist across it. She closed the folder and with a sigh set it apart from the others.

Her office was strategically placed, like a command post, in the centre of the building. There were three wards to the left of her and three to the right. Through observation windows in the office and in each ward she could scan the building at a glance. A similar window in the door commanded the corridor. A row of coloured bulbs on a panel faced her.

She was a slender, well-built woman of forty or more. She had good legs and a brisk manner of walking that was attractive and, at the same time, professional and businesslike. Her legs in a very definite way proclaimed her character. There was sex in them and there was efficiency in them. Her face, on the other hand, served her ill – though it might be truer to say that she served it ill. It was not a bad face – slender, aquiline – but the skin was blotched and pitted, and to cover these defects she resorted to an excess of powder and a very harsh lipstick that gave her the appearance of an experienced courtesan.

Sometime about noon there came a petulant, waspish rasping along the corridor and the deferential hurry of feet. The soothing voice of Nurse Carey poured honey in obeisance, but still it came, a sharp cutting edge, whining like a saw through wood. In the office, Sister Cooney stood up and smoothed down her skirt. She picked up the bundle of folders and opened the door. 'Where would you like to begin today, Doctor?' she enquired without preliminary greeting.

'Nurse will take me round,' Doctor O'Connor-Crowley said briskly.

Sister Cooney handed the charts to Nurse Carey – blonde, young, inexperienced – who took them rather apprehensively.

'By the way,' Sister Cooney began, 'about John Flynn – '

'What about him?'

'I rang earlier and left a message.'

'You know I'm never in at that time. What about him?'

'He died – twenty past ten.'

Doctor O'Connor-Crowley shrugged. 'Well, it was to be expected, wasn't it?'

'Yes.'

'What about new admissions?'

'Two,' Sister Cooney said. 'Ned Hayes back again and – '

'How long has he been out?'

'Six months.'

'Condition?'

'More haemorrhages – not good.'

'Only to be expected,' Doctor O'Connor-Crowley snapped. 'You know his type – insufficient intelligence to stick to a regime. I'm surprised he's been out so long.'

'I put him in Ward 2.'

8

'And the other?'

'Richard Cogley – only nineteen – student – lost a lot of weight – heavy sputum – night sweats – very low.'

'Who sent him in?'

'Doctor O'Driscoll. I had him in with Mr Flynn, but I moved him this morning … before … you know …'

'Yes. Yes. Where's he now?'

'In one of the single rooms down the corridor – number eighteen.'

'I'll see him in the treatment room when I've done the round.'

'I think it mightn't be wise to have him get out of bed.'

'He's not dying is he?'

'He's very weak.'

'Use the wheelchair. Bring along his x-rays. I want to screen him. I can't take the machine to his bedside, you know.'

'Very well,' Sister Cooney said stiffly.

'Well, Nurse, what are we waiting for?' Doctor O'Connor-Crowley turned on her heel.

'Don't call me Ma'am. Call me Doctor,' she said sharply to a raw country youth who complained of chest pains. She took out her stethoscope and sounded him. 'Breathe in. Breathe out. Don't breathe in my face, boy. Turn your head away.'

Doctor O'Connor-Crowley was a short haughty little woman, dressed in dull tweeds, with a sharp 'county' accent and supercilious manner. Her patience, brittle at best, was at its most fragile when dealing with the poor and 'uncouth'. With people of substance and family she could be gracious in a condescending way. But nothing short of the peerage could have made her glow. For the most part she rampaged about, unpredictable as the weather, bringing with her sudden chills, squalls, miasmas.

'Do you want to live?' She glowered at the frightened, hysterical boy.

'Yes, Ma'am – yes, Doctor,' he whined.

'Well, if you do, lie absolutely still – no pillow, mind.'

She turned to the nurse. 'Complete bed rest for this patient.' Then, still within hearing, she added, 'Doesn't the stupid lout realise that his lungs are absolutely riddled with disease!'

'There's a touch of the Dachau mentality about that one,' the schoolmaster Frank O'Shea raged. 'May she roast in hell, the hyphenated hoor!'

In one of the single rooms of the original building lay the foundered wreck of Commander Percy Barnwell, RN (retd).

'And how are we today, Commander?' Doctor O'Connor-Crowley asked graciously, as she glanced at his chart.

'It's this damned climate,' he said fretfully. 'Nothing but fogs and damp and mildew.'

'But it's very bracing today, Commander. Not a fog anywhere.'

'It lingers in the walls, you know.' He pointed. 'Look there at that discoloration.'

'How's the appetite?'

'Completely gone,' the Commander said irritably.

'You must eat, you know.'

'Food has no taste any more.' He pointed to some fruit – grapes, peaches, oranges – in a bowl beside the bed. 'These too. Like bilge water the lot.'

'You are taking the appetiser I gave you?'

'Yes, yes. I took it. Made me sick for days.'

She examined the bottle on his locker. 'It's almost full.'

'I told you it made me sick.'

'You're an impossible patient, Commander.'

'Dry cold air is what we need.' He ignored her. 'And none of your damned nostrums. Davos is the only place. Know a little sanatorium there, high up in the Alps. Dry powered snow. Air

10

as crisp as a biscuit. Damned expensive, though. Too damned expensive. "You must go again," Mildred said to me. "It's your only chance."'

'You know you're not fit to travel as you are,' Doctor O'Connor-Crowley said. 'You must get strong first, and to do that you must eat.'

'It's the climate,' the Commander said again. 'Did you know the ground damp climbs six feet up the walls at Clover Lodge? Mildred tries to keep fires in every room. All the damned timber consumed trying to keep the place heated – and still it climbs.'

'You must eat, Commander.'

'No damp-proof courses,' he said. 'Cost a fortune to rectify now. Original builder skimped on the job. Lazy, dishonest – like most of the tradesmen in this country.'

'We'll have to put you on a high-protein diet. Build you up.'

'Dry air, plenty of rum and warm toddy. That's what I need.'

The doctor looked at him suspiciously. 'No liquor, Commander. You know that. You haven't been … again?'

The Commander stared at her calmly out of his sea-cold eyes and said nothing. He fingered his bristling grey moustache and waited.

'I'm afraid I'll have to ask you to hand over whatever spirits you've got in your locker.'

The Commander shrugged and turned his languid hands palms up on the blankets.

'Nurse, open that locker.'

Nurse Carey hesitated, reluctant to invade his privacy. She looked at him but he gave no indication either of dissent or assent. The doctor stood waiting.

'I'm sorry, Commander,' the nurse whispered as she bent to open the door. His eyes flickered in what might have been amusement, but he said nothing. After a cursory

11

examination, the nurse closed the door and looked up. 'Nothing, Doctor.'

'I'm sorry, Commander, but I had to be sure,' the doctor said by way of apology.

The Commander hugged the bottle between his thighs under the bedclothes. 'I remember being in America during Prohibition,' he said. 'I observed then that the policy was a failure.'

'The circumstances are entirely different,' the doctor replied stiffly.

'It bred evasion and crime,' the Commander went on. 'They had to abandon it in the end.'

'Well, Finn, you cretinous bogman, how are you today?' Arty Byrne said in an affected accent, when he was sure the doctor had gone. He leaped out of bed, ran over to take Vincent Finn's wrist, bent his closely cropped head and consulted his watch. Then, with an exaggerated flourish, Arty brought his wrist closer to his eyes and squinted at the dial again. 'Either this man's dead or my watch is stopped,' he said.

'I know! I know! Groucho Marx!' Vincent laughed.

Arty put on the well-practised leer and ran in a bowed, loping trot back to his bed. He lay there, breathless after his excursion, and fingered his temples thoughtfully, a frown crossing the soft white face that looked like a moon through fog. He ran his fingers up to the crown of his head and felt around for the spot – almost as large as a farthing. He reached into his locker for a hand mirror and held it above him, tilting his head this way and that in an attempt to see it.

'Do you think it *is* going, Vincent?'

'Like feathers from a moulting hen,' Vincent laughed.

'Seriously though?'

'No it's not, you ould cod. If you'd only let it alone, 'twould be all right – instead of washing it every day and clipping it close as a racehorse and massaging it every second minute. Ah, come off it, Arty, you'd have more hair than I have myself, if you'd only forget about it and let it grow.'

'It's going back very far at the temples, all the same.'

The schoolmaster Frank O'Shea, who had been polishing his glasses in the sheet and listening with a smile, thought it was time to put in his oar. 'My poor man,' he said, 'you're worse than you know. Did it ever occur to you what you're really suffering from?'

'What's that? What's that?' Arty turned to him, his round face a study in worry.

'TB of the follicles,' Frank said. He held up his glasses to the light, examining them carefully before putting them on. 'I knew a fellow who suffered from that once, a big strong fellow. Do you know what happened to him?'

'What, Frank? What?' Arty fingered his temples apprehensively.

'Every rib of hair on his body – not just his head, mind, but every blessed rib on his body – fell out.'

'You're coddin',' Arty said. He stared at the schoolmaster to detect the slightest hint of a leg-pull, but could find none.

'And that wasn't the worst of it. The poor fellow went on to develop pronounced female characteristics.' Frank cupped his hands to his chest dramatically. 'Here, for example.'

'Pull the other one, now,' Arty said, but without conviction, because secretly – and this was the source of his worry – he had come to equate possession of hair with virility.

'It didn't stop there,' Frank went on, fingering his nose gravely. 'His behind began to spread and his male parts to shrink and his voice – you should have heard his voice!'

'What happened his voice?' Vincent asked.

13

'Squeaky,' Frank said, 'just like a woman's.'

'That's a hell of a corny story.' Arty was getting more sceptical.

'It ended happily enough,' the schoolmaster said. 'He got a very good job out of it.'

'Go on, you ould cod!' Arty was laughing a little uncertainly. 'Tell us what job he got out of it.'

'A job very suited to his capabilities.' Frank was laughing himself now.

'What job?'

'They made him superintendent of a ladies' lavatory.'

Details of that first morning floated like dust in sunlight.

'You are not to attempt to walk.' Sister Cooney spoke with authority. 'You'll have to learn to accept gracefully that things must be done for you. I told you that when you locked the bathroom door. What do you think would have happened if you had got weak in the bath?'

'I can walk, Nurse,' he said stubbornly.

'But you're not going to,' she said.

She guided him gently but firmly to the wheelchair and he submitted. He knew from the giddiness in his head that she was right, had been right about the bath. But it was not easy to accept that he needed help for such simple things – not easy to accept that he was a patient and in the hands of others. It gave a status and importance to his illness that he was reluctant to concede.

In the treatment room Doctor O'Connor-Crowley was waiting, her stethoscope hanging from her neck. 'Well,' she said, as Sister Cooney helped him to the couch, 'you're in a pretty state, aren't you!' She signalled to the sister to remove his pyjama top, and began to examine him, first with the stethoscope and then with her fingers. She placed one hand flat on his chest and tapped it with the fingers of the other. She did the same with his back, listening carefully as she tapped, like a builder testing for hidden cavities.

The treatment room smelled of ether and disinfectant. It was an uncomfortable, clinical, cold place with steel filing cabinets and a silver-coloured sterilising unit that simmered and steamed. In one corner was a machine with electric wires trailing from it. The front was a blue-tinted adjustable screen at chest level, behind which he was assisted by Sister Cooney. The light in the room was switched off and the machine switched on. The glow from the screen threw a lurid reflection on the doctor, who sat on a high stool and tilted the screen this way and that and hummed thoughtfully to herself. Then she switched it off and called for light. Sister Cooney helped him on with his pyjama top and led him to the couch. His legs felt like wasted rubber and he was glad of the opportunity to sit. There was a cold sweat on his face and he shivered. Through his thin frame the bones of his bottom projected onto the hard couch and he shifted in discomfort.

The doctor prepared a syringe while Sister Cooney rolled up his sleeve and knotted a rubber tube round his biceps.

'We'll do a BSR,' the doctor said.

He watched as she prepared to plunge in the needle. She stopped as she was about to make the insertion, seized his chin between thumb and forefinger and turned it firmly from her. 'Look the other way.'

When the blood sample had been taken and set standing in a tall tube, she opened a thin file and studied it. 'Sputum test on the fifteenth – positive. Sister, see that he has another taken and sent away in the morning.' She sat behind a table and studied him thoughtfully for a few moments before she spoke. 'So, Richard Cogley, here you are.'

There didn't seem to be a reply that he could profitably make to this and he remained silent.

'You're a student, I see. What do you study?'

'Engineering, Doctor.'

'Well,' she said bluntly, 'you can put engineering out of your mind for the foreseeable future.'

'How long …?' he began.

'You're here a day and you're asking how long,' she said impatiently. 'It's clear that whatever you may know about engineering, you know nothing about the nature of this disease.'

'Doctor O'Driscoll said three months …'

She stroked her chin. Three months, three weeks, who could say exactly how long this unfortunate young man had to live. His left lung was certainly in a mess and there was something suspicious also in the apex of the right.

'We'll see,' she said dismissively. 'A great deal depends on yourself. I'm putting you on strict bed rest. You must lie absolutely still. No sitting up, except for meals. No reading either. Absolute rest is what you need. Sister, ring for Nurse Carey to take him back. I want to speak to you alone for a moment.'

As the door closed behind him he could hear her voice raised in anger. 'Why wasn't I told about the condition of this patient? He's much too ill to be moved unnecessarily.'

'I did tell you,' he heard Sister Cooney protest.

'Nonsense, Sister!'

Then he was whisked away and there was nothing but the click of the wheel bearings and the silken whisper of Nurse Carey's thighs brushing together.

16

2

Long before visiting time Lily Moore was sitting up eagerly in bed, her hair, which she had washed the previous night, freshly set, the brown strands sparkling with hidden fire. She had put on her bra, her best yellow nightie, and the lime bed jacket she had crocheted with such care for his coming – the hooked needle looping in and out, drawing the wool into an intricate pattern, like the strands of love drawing their lives together.

She had put on a little green eye shadow and spread it evenly with her finger, and a pale orange lipstick, thinning it out towards the corners where her lips seemed overripe. She had dabbed her mouth with tissue to take off the surplus and spent a long time viewing herself in the hand mirror. She practised smiling, watching herself critically as she did so. What she was aiming for was a certain cool charm, underlaid with mystery. She damped down the ardent flame on her cheekbones with a little pale powder, then scented herself lightly behind the ears, at the throat, on either side of the neck, on the palms of each hand and in the cleft between her breasts.

When the first surge of visitors came, she sparkled effervescently, greeting the people she had come to know so well – Mrs Doran's husband, fingering his hat uncertainly, as his feet, more

17

used to striding across ploughland, edged cautiously over the waxed floor; her friend Elsie's father and mother; Annie Murphy's brother, whose admiring looks were like a seal on her preparations. Then her mother came, a warm, worried woman, who kissed her and admired her bed jacket and told her she had a little too much make-up on for a young girl like her, but looked nice all the same and very well too, and enquired if she was feeling better and eating better, and how the cough was and what the doctor had said.

Lily told her about the new treatment they were planning for her, which meant she was getting better because it was only when you were getting better that it could be given. It meant putting air in somewhere between the ribs and collapsing part of the lung to give it a rest, and there was a big needle and the thought of it wasn't very pleasant, but it had to be done and would help to get her out of there quicker.

Her mother gave her family news and neighbours' news and intimate women's news and every other kind of news except the news she wanted to hear, and that was odd because Joe lived just down the road and the world revolved around Joe – which her mother knew very well, because everyone knew that she and Joe were as good as engaged and had been in and out of each other's houses since they were children and in love with each other since that time too.

'Joe is coming today, you know,' Lily ventured.

'Are you sure?' Her mother looked at her anxiously. 'Did he write to you?'

'You know Joe,' Lily smiled indulgently. 'He's not used to writing letters. Give me a spanner, he'd say, and let me at a car and I'll work at it all day, but don't ask me to take a pen in my hand. You remember when he went to work in the garage and we all said a fellow with his education should try for a job in the

18

office, or train to be a sales manager, but that wouldn't suit Joe at all.'

'An office job would be cleaner,' her mother said.

'Everybody should do what he wants to do and never mind what other people say,' Lily replied.

Her mother's look became troubled. 'Most people do what they want to do anyway – in the end,' she said. 'They can't be forced. Remember that about life, girl, and you'll never be too disappointed when somebody does something you don't expect him to do. People only do what they must. They follow their nature in the long run.'

'Disappointed?' Lily asked. 'About Joe, you mean? Why would I be disappointed?'

'Did you write to him?'

'The very minute I was allowed visitors – apart from the family – I wrote and told him it was all right to come, and today's the day.'

'Some people won't come near this place, you know that?' her mother said.

'Joe's not like that!' Lily was shocked.

'Some people hardly talk to me any more,' her mother went on. 'Women I've known all my life – Mrs Hegarty, for instance. Crosses to the other side when she sees me coming and just nods. People can be very queer about things like this.'

'Joe's not that kind.' Lily was beginning to get annoyed with her mother and her equation of Joe with silly women like Mrs Hegarty, whom she had never liked anyway.

'People change,' her mother said.

Lily looked keenly at her and spoke in a flat voice from which all feeling had been drained. 'You think Joe's changed, is that it?'

Her mother reached out for Lily's hand – the nails carefully

19

lacquered – and squeezed it. 'I don't know, child. Three months is a long time to some people.'

'He'll come. You'll see.' Lily thought it was unlike her mother to be so pessimistic.

'Joe is the outdoor type. All he thinks about is cars and speed. He's never been a day sick in his life. You can't expect him to know anything about sickness, not to talk of … TB.'

'What are you trying to do, Mammy, anyway?' Uncertainty, doubt, the beginning of fear was in Lily's voice.

'I don't want to see you hurt, child. I can't help hearing things. Your brother Sean … '

'What did Sean say? Did Joe say something to him?'

'Joe doesn't talk much to Sean anymore. He always seems to be in too much of a hurry.'

'What did Sean say?' There was panic in Lily's voice now.

'Don't ask me any more, Lily. He won't come. That's all I know.'

Lily drooped in the bed like a crumpled flower, the animated certainties of her face collapsing into incomprehension.

There was concern and love and shared suffering in the squeeze of her mother's hand. 'Don't, girl. Dry your eyes.' The fierce urge to protect her daughter made her want to cry herself.

'What did Sean say?'

Her mother hesitated, then tried to create a diversion by reaching for her basket on the floor. 'I brought you something nice.'

'I want to know, Mammy.'

Her mother sighed and rocked the basket on her lap, as if she were soothing a child. 'You know boys,' she said vaguely. 'One thing today and something else tomorrow. Always changing.'

'Are you talking about Sean or Joe?'

'They're all the same, girl: new ideas, new friends – chopping and changing, trying everything on for size, like someone trying on coats in a shop – never satisfied, because they're always afraid there's something better someplace else, something exciting going on that they'll miss, always in a mad hurry to live all their lives in a minute and forgetting ... ' Her voice dropped away into silence and she gestured helplessly with her hands.

'Forgetting their ... friends?' Lily whispered.

Her mother nodded sadly.

'And making new ones?'

Her mother nodded again.

Lily felt her weak control buckle in the face of the torrent that her next question let loose inside her. 'Girl friends?'

Her mother stroked her hand and looked at the floor. 'That's what Sean says.'

'I hate him!' Lily hissed vehemently. 'Tell Sean I hate him for his spying and his lies.'

'Sean told me not to tell you,' her mother said quietly. 'He wouldn't want to hurt you, love. Sean was very cut up when you came in here. Did you know that? He's not himself at all since it happened.' She dabbed her eyes with her glove. 'None of us are.' She moved her chair in closer and bent forward to shield Lily's heaving body from view. 'Hush, child,' she said. 'Hush, now.'

Jack Carbery had no family and no one to visit him. Occasionally he picked up the overflow from another bed – the kindly who meant well and asked about his length of stay and his prospects of release, the bored who had squeezed whatever drama they could out of their immediate friend or relative and looked to him for some sensational revelation that might bolster up their sagging afternoon, the Cheerful Charlies who told him he was bursting and lucky to be inside, out of the weather and the world's rough edge. The irony of this was never lost on Jack, because for him it was only too true. He was one of those chronic patients with calcified lesions that occasionally showed signs of softening but never totally broke down. He would be admitted and spend a few weeks on bed rest, then be placed on graded exercise and discharged after a few months.

For Jack the real problems of life began on his discharge. He was alone in the world and depended on the charity of the family with whom he had worked for most of his life. To him the sanatorium was a cosy billet, where he found good food, a soft bed, and could live indolently – running errands for the staff, collecting letters for the post, and doing the daily shopping for the other patients.

On visiting days, Jack, a dark solitary man with a sharp nose and unfathomable eyes, ticked through the racing page with the stub of a pencil and marked his fancy, and listened. Outside, the shouting of children – who were not admitted – as they raced over the lawns. Inside, strange faces and random conversation. Behind the screen of his newspaper, Jack strained, his ears extracting from the babel some snatch that interested him.

'... Your Aunt Nellie was in a terrible state when she heard. Said we should have told everybody you were gone to work in England. But they'd know before long, anyway, with half the country in here ...'

The social stigma of having the disease meant nothing to Carbery. It was not having it sufficiently badly, or worse still, the prospect of a full recovery that appalled him.

'... That man over there, is he bad? Him with the paper. Don't let him see you lookin'. Is he here long? ...'

Carbery smiled thinly behind his paper. People were always asking questions like that. How long was it this time? He remembered his last discharge – the mysterious chest pains he had developed when the time came near. Had they been real, or just imaginary as the doctor had insisted? And the blood flecks in his sputum? He had found that if he coughed long and hard enough, they came. From the irritated membrane of his throat, from his lungs – who could tell? But they were hardly a sign of perfect health.

'… Mike Lannon came with us. You know Mike? He's a third cousin of your own. But he wouldn't come up. Nothing would persuade him to come inside the door.'

'What ails him?'

'Afraid he'd pick up something, what else! He said to tell you he was asking for you.'

'Tell him not to bother. He might do himself an injury …'

Doctor O'Connor-Crowley had been sent for and she had come irritably, her voice filing away the iron silence, to stand by his bed and glare and roar, 'Well, Carbery, malingering time again, eh?'

'No, Doctor, no. I took a sudden turn.'

'A sudden turn out the door and down the avenue – that's the turn you're going to take.'

'I think my lung is going to collapse.'

'We'll soon see about that.' She had whipped out her stethoscope, while the nurse bared his chest. 'Breathe in. Breathe out. Turn your face away, man. There! Just as I thought. Sound as a bell.'

He had protested, making his most effective arguments out of long, racking coughs, smothering off into breathlessness. Eventually, because she had not dared risk making a mistake, he had been allowed to stay – but only at a price.

'Complete bed rest for this patient,' she had roared. 'Take away his pillows at once. If, as he fears, his lung is in danger of collapse, we shall have to put him on blocks. Nurse, have two six-inch blocks standing by to raise the foot of his bed, if required.'

She had examined the brown stains on his clubbed fingers. 'Aha! Smoking – I thought as much! Carbery, hand over your cigarettes and pipe at once. If I hear of you sitting upright in that bed, much less smoking, I'll have you thrown out instantly.'

Then she was off to prescribe some placebo, chosen solely for its nastiness, and in this way she had harried him, until he gave in and took himself off down the avenue with his few belongings in a cardboard case, and made his way to the farmhouse, about ten miles off, where there had been no great welcome for him either.

'Here comes Céline!' Vincent called.

Arty ran his hand nervously over his hair and leaned forward. 'Lucky brute that Hubert,' he said.

A trim young woman pushed through the door, a knitted beret set at a provocative angle on her dark, swinging hair. Her bold glance, suggesting a deep knowledge of men, stirred a primitive response. Eyes swivelled as she moved, rump a wiggle, through the ward.

'Some woman!' Vincent sighed as the door closed behind her – sighed as he had sighed every Sunday afternoon when she came to visit her husband. Through the glass partition they watched the weekly ritual unfold.

Hubert, ex-British Army sergeant – neat moustache, erect carriage – sat in his bed, arms outstretched to greet her. Hubert, they agreed, was something of a fraud and didn't deserve such a beautiful girl. His name, like his English accent, was an affectation. His critics – less flamboyant men, who had known him in his early days when he was plain Har Kelly, milk roundsman – scorned the metamorphosed Hubert O'Kelley, military strategist, indispensable prop of the Imperial General Staff. After the war he had been detailed to France to repatriate the bodies of

24

British troops killed in action there, and he had returned with TB and an exotic wife – the delectable Céline.

They watched as she flung herself into his arms.

'Women are what we need,' Vincent cried, 'exciting, pliant women.'

'Opening like flowers to be pollinated.' Arty took up the chant.

'Mysterious eastern women in yashmaks, educated in the arts of love.'

'Harem women in transparent draperies –'

'Courtesans, concubines, wantons, loose, lascivious, amorous women –'

'Artists' models, posing in the nude on soft leopard skins –'

'Blonde, Nordic women, coming like Venus from the sea –'

'Tiny drops of water glistening on their body hair –'

'Cool to touch –'

'And salty to taste –'

'God! What we need is women –'

'To lie in the sun and be smothered in white drifts of nakedness –'

'Legs and thighs and breasts –'

'Stop it!' Arty cried. 'You're driving me mad.' He lay back and wondered if he were normal. He had heard Frank say – but you could never be sure when Frank was being serious – that the disease was an aphrodisiac. He found it hard to imagine that Frank was plagued with the kind of fantasies that came floating into his own mind – tantalising visions of honey-coloured women spread on beds, tumbling, rolling, teasing women, smelling of musk and jasmine, moving in on him, until there was nothing else in the world to see and touch and scent and taste, and he felt himself sink away and drown in seas of flesh.

Phil Turner lay in bed with his hands clasped behind his bald head and listened to their conversation with growing distaste.

He was a big moist man with wet lips and hot evasive eyes. He was forever trying to establish physical contact with people and forever being rebuffed. He had a way of laying his steamy palm on people's shoulders, around boys' necks or on their knees that caused them to shiver and shrug him off in disgust without ever knowing exactly why they found contact with him so distasteful. He took rebuffs humbly – and tried again as soon as the opportunity presented itself. His very humility was offensive.

Phil began talking now in his soft throaty voice – a voice that seemed to savour and relish words and part with them reluctantly, as if he were engaged in fellatio with language. 'You should see them in Brittas Bay in the summer,' he said, 'naked and shameless young ones with nothing between them and the world only a little wisp of cloth.'

'So that's how you spent your Sundays,' Frank laughed, 'lying in the sand dunes, spying on the women.'

'It's a scandal in a Christian country, that's what it is,' Phil said.

'I must go to this Brittas Bay when I get out,' Arty said. 'Where did you say it is, Phil?'

'Disgusting! that's what it is,' Phil said vehemently. 'Like that shameless one in there.'

They turned eagerly to look. Through the window they saw Céline, her skirts riding high as she sat on Hubert's lap. She had nail scissors in her hand and was trimming his moustache, giggling and whispering and kissing as she trimmed.

'We used swim in the river, a crowd of us together with nothing on,' Vincent said, one eye hungrily on those rising skirts.

'A crowd of young fellows going in together is a different thing entirely,' Phil said.

'That would suit you, all right.' Frank laughed.

'That's enough of that, now!' Phil turned away crossly, put his head down and pulled up the blankets, a fashion he had when the conversation went against him.

People's tolerance of Phil wore out quickly, so he was always on the look out for new friends. No sooner was a patient admitted than Phil was round to sit on his bed and shake hands. Shaking hands was an obsession with him. His limp palm, forever extended, went before him, questing wetly for flesh to press. He would seize some inexperienced young hand in his flabby grip and draw it and its owner ever nearer to himself, while he fixed him with his dilated, hypnotic eyes and washed him in a lather of flattery.

Boys – except for the occasional one who sensed in Phil's need some desperate echo of his own – learned quickly to be chary of him. Though there was a rule against it, they learned to lock the bathroom door before stepping into the bath. The sight of that moist face looking in from the softly-opened door, the tongue feeling tentatively over the fat lips, and the ingratiating offer to come in and wash their backs was enough to put them on their guard. Phil, who was in no sense a violent man and accepted rebuffs readily, like a dog which expects no better, would withdraw immediately on the first sign of alarm. But he was ever the optimist and people learned never to be surprised at hearing him padding about outside, pawing the door and quietly turning the knob.

When Céline wiggled out again, Vincent watched her compulsively, his imagination trapped in the undertow of those sinful, Gallic legs. Though he didn't know it then, it was the last he was to see of her. Within a week Hubert would be on his way to an army convalescent home in England and she would take that provocative body off to sabotage the morals of more fortunate men elsewhere. When the door had closed behind her and all that was left was the scent of her passing, he held up in disgust between thumb and forefinger the letter he had been reading. 'God!' he exclaimed. 'To think of women like that and then – this!'

'I know!' Arty said. 'Pen friends are all a cod anyway.'

'Listen to it.' Vincent affected a gushing, girlish voice:

and then we went to this wonderful picture with Jeanette MacDonald and Nelson Eddy – he's a lovely singer, isn't he, and so handsome? – and it had lovely songs in it about Maytime and apple blossom, and it was so sad and nice that I cried …

'Are you sure you're mature enough to handle a woman like that?' Arty teased. 'That big stooge, Nelson Eddy!' he mocked. 'Dressed like a Mounty – that's the one, isn't it? – out in the middle of nowhere, singing 'When I'm Calling You' with full orchestra and chorus coming out of the rocks. I tell you what, your one is living dangerously.'

'Will I write and ask her – just for the cod – if she's ever had it?'

'Had what?'

'You know very well what.'

'A one like that!' Arty cried scornfully. 'Of course she hasn't – nor her mother either.'

28

3

How long had he lain there? Three weeks? Two months? He couldn't be sure. Time was just a blurring or brightening of light, a murmuring or a silence in the corners of the room, a changing pattern on the ceiling. He remembered, once, stumbling along a lighted corridor, determined to reach the bathroom and being steered back again and firmly scolded by Sister Cooney. He remembered the humiliation of the bedpan, and the urine bottle that inexplicably spilled in his fumbling fingers, the repeated changing of sheets and the kindness that was worse than any rebuke.

He had rallied and had been lucid enough for a day or two, but after that, a gradual drifting down into some twilight zone where coughing beat about him like a great wind and existence was reduced to reaching for the disgusting sputum mug and drooling into it thick pulpy matter that he dared not examine for fear it should confirm his suspicion that he was spewing out disintegrating lung tissue.

He remembered his mother's face bending anxiously over him. He remembered the pressure of her hand on his as she sat whispering in the sick silence. His father's troubled eyes turning away to stare out the window, because men were expected to suppress emotion. His father remarking in an unnatural voice on the height they were above the river. His father carrying him on his shoulders through the summer fields, the air a drift of pollen and sweet smells, the collie racing ahead to turn in the cows. The others, too, floated in and out of his vision, a blur of light about them like a photograph out of focus. Eileen and Michael – but not Liam. Where was Liam?

He remembered Eileen feeding him pieces of orange, the scent of her hands stronger than the fruit, her fingertips soft on his lips, her black hair fragrant about him as she kissed his forehead. Were those her tears on his cheek? That day his father had carried him had been her third birthday – a fat little thing with ringlets, putting her doll to sleep, and they had fought because he had wanted to take her up and feed her. In the morning they had gone about in the green sunshine, listening for cockling hens in the glistening straw, and carried the warm eggs into the cool gloom of the kitchen, where his mother arranged them in a lengthening line along the dresser. What was it about cockling hens that was so magical, so matutinal, so suffused with sunlight and summer freshness?

Sometimes a grey, military-looking man in plaid dressing gown shuffled in to stand at the end of the bed and look at him kindly and ask, 'How are you today, old chap?' Once he had come tiptoeing conspiratorially with his hand in his pocket, withdrawing it to disclose a medicine glass. 'A little something to warm you up,' he had said and propped him up and held the glass to his lips. The spirits were fiery in his throat and afterwards he had lain in a fuzzy haze and felt the heat course through him and his head grow dizzy, and later still, he had slept and woken in a steam of sweat, his head throbbing.

Sister Cooney, starched and fresh, bustling about the room, smiling through a vermilion gash, her eyes kindly as she rearranged the pillows, tucked in the blankets. Soft jut of her breasts as she leaned over him. The purposeful click of her heels on the corridor.

A tall emaciated man with a sad drooping face and gapped yellow teeth came at nightfall to sprinkle holy water on his forehead. He spoke parsimoniously – when he spoke at all – a few meagre syllables about the weather or someone who had died, with no detectable difference in his manner, whatever the topic.

Imperceptibly he had learned to divine, without being told, when death was in the place. It began with a flurry on the corridor, an urgent coming and going of many feet. This was followed by a tiptoeing silence. Sister Cooney and the staff, if they came at all, seemed abstracted and withdrawn, hurrying off immediately, dispensing with the niceties of tidying the bed or straightening the locker. Then the door was closed and there came the heavy trundling of a trolley down the corridor. The lift gates clanged and clashed. The motor whirred. Then silence, a prolonged hush that outlasted the reopening of the door; and for the rest of the day, a solemnity, a bleakness, a darkness spreading like a stain, a feeling of being trapped in some ineluctable destiny, grinding towards ruin.

Lily sat waiting outside the treatment room on the male floor, her hands demurely in her lap, looking down at the waxed brown floor-covering, seeing, without being particularly aware of them, depressions caused by sharp heels or the steel point of an umbrella. She made a conscious effort not to think, to suspend herself in an abstraction of medicated brownness, immersing herself in sight and smell. Thinking, remembering, anticipating – all were painful. The anxious flutter of her stomach clamoured for attention every time the sound of voices came from behind the door.

Ever since her mother's visit, Lily had contracted in on herself like a sensitive plant that recoils when touched. She cried constantly, spoke little, ate less. She woke in the morning with the dull sense of loss and the futility of the new day. She drifted at night through racking tears into dreams where huge shadows menaced her peace. Waking to momentary relief, she was soon conscious of her isolation, a tiny figure stranded on the edge of some dark universe, loveless and alone. She felt the need to be embraced into a warm comforting humanity and cried again, remembering her mother's arms and the large reassurance of her father. Childhood was such a simple time, when love was constant and one's need of it did not reach beyond family.

When the door opened, she was near to tears again. A young man of about her own age came out, swathed in a beige dressing gown that was too large for him. He looked at her curiously, and seeing her distress, smiled sympathetically.

'Your first time?' he asked.

She nodded her head without saying anything, and they were poised there for a moment looking at each other. She noted his pale face and the black hair hanging dankly on his forehead.

'It's nothing much, really. You won't feel a thing.'

She nodded again.

'You have a little fullness here.' He pointed to his chest. 'That's all.'

The young nurse who had brought Lily up in the lift came out. 'Back to your ward, now, Vincent,' she said, 'and, Lily, you may come in.'

Vincent hitched up his dressing gown, tightened the belt and appealed to the nurse. 'There's nothing to it, Nurse Lambert, is there?'

'I keep telling her that,' the nurse said.

'The first hundred years are the worst,' Vincent smiled ruefully and turned to go.

Inside, Nurse Lambert helped Lily off with her dressing gown and eased her into the required position on the couch. She lay on her right side and waited, her body tensed and stiff.

'Well, Lily,' Doctor Staples spoke kindly behind her, 'how are you feeling?'

'All right, Doctor.' She felt her mouth embarrassingly dry and licked her lips.

Doctor Staples, who was the county medical officer, came on Tuesdays and Fridays. He arrived in the afternoon and spent the rest of the day in the place. From the moment his car was seen coming up the avenue until his departure, Ardeevan was a ferment of speculation and rumour. He was the one who was responsible for admissions and discharges. For an hour he was closeted with charts and reports. Then he emerged to make a thorough round, giving news of sputum tests and x-rays, prescribing new treatment, discontinuing the old, encouraging the faint-hearted, weeding out rootless optimism, walking thoughtfully away – his dark head bent – from the bed of someone whose case was beyond remedy.

He was a handsome man in a sallow, Latin way and caused a good deal of Byronic flutter on the female floor.

'Now, I'll tell you what I'm going to do,' he said, 'and how you can help me – and help yourself at the same time.'

Lily tensed herself into a tighter knot as she felt his hands lifting aside the jacket of her pyjamas and exposing her back.

'These are your ribs.' He probed gently over them, counting them, feeling for the gaps between. 'What I'm going to do is put some air into the cavity between your lung and the chest wall. Do you understand that?'

'Yes, Doctor,' Lily quavered.

'Now, you can help me by relaxing. Imagine you're very tired. You've had an exhausting day and you come home and just flop on the bed. Can you do that?'

'I'll try.'

'Good girl! That's better.'

His hands moved over her ribs, probing more strongly, feeling for the intercostal spaces. He beckoned to the nurse who handed him a swab which he dabbed lightly on Lily's skin. The coldness of it made her shiver and stiffen again.

'Relax, Lily. Just a little prick, now, when I give you the anaesthetic.'

Lily felt the thin searing burn of the needle deep in her flesh. Then with a sudden clean movement it was out again.

'That's the worst of it over,' he reassured her. 'In a few minutes the area will be numb and you'll feel nothing at all.'

He kept up a line of inconsequential chatter while he waited, now and again laying his finger lightly on her back to test her reaction. When he was satisfied that it was safe to proceed, he beckoned to Nurse Lambert who handed him a long hollow needle in a kidney dish.

'Now, Lily, relax again.'

As Lily went limp he pressed suddenly between her ribs with the fingers of one hand, broke the skin with a swift thrust of the needle that he held in the other and plunged it home. 'There, now, that wasn't bad, was it?'

'Are you going to – begin?' Lily asked apprehensively.

Doctor Staples laughed and patted her arm. 'It's in. Just hold still and we'll have you back in your bed in no time.'

She lay there, the nurse lightly holding her arm and shoulder, while he hooked her up to the air machine and studied the gauges.

'That should be enough for a start,' he said after a few minutes.

34

When the machine was unhooked, the nurse handed him a swab which he pressed firmly to Lily's back, withdrawing the needle at the same time with swift dexterity. He held the swab tightly over the puncture for a few seconds and then lifted it. 'Some light dressing, Nurse,' he said.

'It's a little like putting a broken leg in plaster and giving it a chance to mend,' he told Lily. 'How are you feeling?'

'Fine!' Lily said bravely. But as soon as she lifted her shoulders from the couch a fullness and a giddiness beset her. Her chest on the left side burned and her vision began to blur at the edges.

'Lie down again,' Doctor Staples said, seeing her distress. 'You may expect some discomfort for a while. But it will pass. We'll have you taken back to your ward. Nurse, bring the trolley, please. Relax, Lily. You'll be all right in a day or two.'

Commander Barnwell, moustache bristling, leaned forward from his prop of pillows and faced Doctor Staples. 'What's this damned artificial whatever-you-call-it, then?'

'Artificial pneumoperitoneum,' Doctor Staples said with a quiet determination not to be outstared or downfaced. 'It's a question of introducing air into the peritoneal cavity –'

'I'm damned if anybody's going to monkey about with my insides!' The Commander fixed him with his cold eyes.

'It's only a very minor operation,' Doctor Staples explained patiently.

'Won't hear of it!' The Commander was inflexible. 'It's against my principles. I'm a – Christian Scientist. We don't hold with things like that.'

Doctor Staples consulted his chart. 'It says here you're Church of England.'

'I'm a C. of E. Christian Scientist,' the Commander maintained stoutly. 'A man has a right, even in this goddamned country, to follow whatever religion he wants to, hasn't he?'

'You believe in faith healing, then?' Doctor Staples asked without attempting to hide his scepticism.

'I'll put it this way,' the Commander countered testily. 'I don't believe in tinkering with a man's engineering. When I go down, I intend to go with all my plates intact.'

'Well,' Doctor Staples said with resignation, 'no need to make a decision today. Think it over, Commander. It's for your own good, you know.'

'Fresh dry air,' the Commander said, 'plenty of sunshine, good food, brown bread – nothing like it.'

'The sooner we begin treatment the better,' Doctor Staples advised.

Commander Barnwell ignored him. 'South Africa, I'm told, is a fine country. Good climate. Pull round there in no time. Bit of trouble with the Kaffirs, I dare say, but you can't have everything.'

Doctor Staples shook his head angrily as he withdrew. 'He's a tough old bastard. I've a good mind to fling him out if he doesn't accept treatment. Let him go to South Africa.'

'Rambling the poor man is,' Sister Cooney said. 'If it's not South Africa, it's Switzerland or California. He was in Switzerland for a while until the money ran out. They're in a poor way, you know.'

'I suspected that. I had quite a job to persuade him to come in here in the first place, until I explained to the wife that under the new Health Act, treatment was free for everyone.'

'It's poor land out there at Clover Lodge and a big tumble-down house with huge rates on it. All he seems to do is keep a few horses and sell off the timber.'

'You know the place, then?' He looked at Sister Cooney in mild surprise, as if he had never before considered that she might have an existence and an ambience beyond the walls of the sanatorium.

'Yes. I come from out that way.'

'Right!' Doctor Staples said with a sudden briskness that indicated he had heard enough of the matter. 'Get on to him again about that APP. Get him used to the idea. Get someone who's on it to ramble in and talk to him. How about O'Connor-Crowley? Could she persuade him?'

'She'd be like a red rag to a bull.'

'Oh! I thought she might be on the one wavelength. County – and all!' He smiled satirically at Sister Cooney, knowing her antipathy.

'I think I might have a word with his wife,' Sister Cooney said. 'She seems to be the only one who has any influence with him.'

'Do that,' Doctor Staples said.

Mildred Barnwell came every Sunday. She sat beside her husband's bed, a long, melancholy, mildewed woman, like a fading geranium. She answered his questions about the land and the crumbling house, hearing, as he went on with his predictable catechism, the sound of her own feet through the deserted rooms, smelling again the musty dampness that clung even yet to her bottle-green cardigan, to the cold moistness of her skin. She held a cigarette in a black holder between her first and second finger and blew smoke from round thin lips.

'Poor darling,' she said, 'it would be rather painful, wouldn't it?'

'Rot!' the Commander said crossly, his mind on the war and U-boats surfacing out of the grey mists of the Atlantic. What did the woman know about such things as pain and danger? What could anyone know who hadn't gone through the hell

37

of gunfire and torpedoes, of menacing submarines and cold heaving seas?

His wife looked at him shrewdly, weighing him up, knowing the intricate workings of his mind, deliberately laying herself out like a carpet over which he might stamp in anger in the direction she desired. A flicker of affectionate concern showed briefly in her face as she turned aside to drop the ash from her cigarette into the ashtray on the locker. 'I don't like the idea,' she said dogmatically.

'You don't have to,' the Commander said. 'They're not your lungs.'

'We don't even know if the thing will do any good,' she persisted.

'Must give the fellow credit for knowing his job, dammit!' the Commander replied testily.

'I don't like it,' she said again.

There was a knock on the door and a pleasant, rather magnificent woman in her forties looked in.

'It's the bishop's wife,' Mrs Barnwell whispered.

'May I come in?'

'My dear Mrs Mc Candle,' Mrs Barnwell rose to greet her, 'how wonderful to see you! Do come in.'

Mrs Mc Candle closed the door and came forward, smiling, with her hand outstretched. Her black hair curved softly about her handsome face. Looking at her, the Commander marvelled, not for the first time, at the strange chemistry that had brought the bishop and herself together.

'How are you, Commander?' she said.

'Fine!' he said. 'How's the bishop?'

'A bit tired after the synod last week. You know how he expends himself. He's just down the corridor having a word with that young Watchorn boy. He'll be along presently.'

What was it, the Commander wondered, that had induced a woman of her calibre, a warm, sensual, hedonistic-looking woman, to waste herself on such a dried-up, musty theological treatise as the bishop? Or was he seriously underestimating the man? The thought that he might be intrigued him.

'Yes,' the bishop's wife was saying, 'we always call in here when Eric comes on visitation to the Reverend Smirkin. Eric likes to keep in touch. One rather gets the feeling at the best of times that we are a beleaguered minority and it must be even worse for anyone in here. There aren't many of our persuasion in the hospital, are there, Commander?'

'Haven't a notion,' the Commander said with indifference.

'Well, there's the Watchorn boy,' his wife said, 'and poor Willie Whitehead. You've heard of him? Very sad. In and out of hospital for the past fifteen years.'

'Poor man!' the bishop's wife said. 'We must get Eric to call on him.'

There was a knock on the door and Mrs Barnwell opened it to admit a frail little man in a grey suit and clerical collar. His shrunk shanks were bound tightly in ecclesiastical gaiters, which gave him an absurd, knock-kneed appearance when he walked.

'Ah, Bishop Mc Candle,' Mrs Barnwell said.

There were greetings and handshakes all round. As he held the bishop's dry bony fingers in his the Commander had difficulty again in reconciling his ascetic air of scrubbed holiness with the rich and ample charms of Mrs McCandle. Perhaps there was some intellectual excitement about the man, some sexuality of power that attracted her. On the surface, at least, they seemed a devoted couple.

'Smirkin is a regular visitor, I understand,' the bishop said.

'Yes, he looks in occasionally,' the Commander agreed without much enthusiasm.

'Capable man,' the bishop said. 'Devoted pastor. We need more like him in the ministry.'

'He does rather go on a bit in the pulpit, I always think,' Mrs Barnwell protested mildly.

'Fine theologian,' the bishop countered. 'Very sound on the Trinity.'

Now that they've done their duty, why can't they go, the Commander thought sourly. He searched about in his mind for something shocking to say that would make them withdraw in well-bred confusion. But he daren't say it. Mildred would never forgive him for it. If he was a little younger and more robust, he might set himself to seduce the bishop's wife. But Mildred could hardly be expected to forgive him for that either. Though one never knew with Mildred. She had forgiven him for a lot in her day. That was her strength – her capacity to forgive.

'Well, Lavinia, my dear,' the bishop was saying at last, 'we must be on our way.' He shook hands a second time. 'It's such a pleasure to have met you both again,' he said, 'though one could have wished it were in happier circumstances.'

'I do hope to see you out and about again soon.' Mrs Mc Candle took the Commander's moist hand in her own plump, well-manicured one.

The Commander pressed her fingers firmly and held on to them sufficiently long for her to look at him with a little start of surprise and withdraw her hand hurriedly.

'Perhaps a little prayer before we go,' the bishop suggested. He stood beside the bed, his face level with the Commander's eyes, joined his hands and intoned solemnly: 'O Lord, look down with favour on Thy servant, Percival. Comfort him in his affliction. By the gift of Thy holy healing restore him, if such be Thy will, to his pristine health. Imbue him and us with a love of Thy word, and gather us at the end of our

40

mortal journey into the bosom of Thy mercy for all eternity. Amen.'

A little less of that gathering for another while, the Commander thought, as they left. That was the curse of all clerics. They were so ready to promise obedience and resignation on behalf of people who, if they were left to themselves, would probably turn to the Creator and say: 'Lord, there's only one thing you can do for me that would really please me. Don't take me until I'm ready to go. I'm not ready now and I don't expect to be ready in the foreseeable future. But I promise to think about it one day. So until then, give me good health, prosperity and friends to share it with.'

He looked at Mildred who had resumed her seat. The old girl was worried about him. He had known what she was at well enough with her taking a stand against the doctor. At least he had begun to suspect. Perhaps he should – to please her. There was nobody else to please, except himself, and he had done that most of his life. The habit of a lifetime was too ingrained to break easily, however. There would have to be some quid pro quo – some compromise. He thought of the empty bottle stuffed into an old sock in his locker.

If Mildred cared enough about him, he could strike a hard bargain. He looked at her speculatively, then reached out his hand and let it fall lightly on hers where it lay along the armrest of her chair.

4

After tea and between the changes of staff, there was a quiet hour, when patients who were well enough – and some who weren't well at all – visited their friends. It was a time for sitting on beds, playing draughts or cards and gossiping. For the young it was a time for adventure and romance.

Elsie Hogan, who never missed an opportunity for either, was out on the verandah, humming a little tune, proclaiming to anyone who cared to know on the male floor that she was accessible. There were limitations in her position of which she was well aware. It wasn't easy to present her charms to anyone who could only have a crow's view of her. Besides, her buff hospital dressing gown hid, without any saving hint of mystery, what scheming woman has always found it politic to – at the very least – half reveal.

She waved vaguely to a middle-aged man smoking a contemplative pipe at the other end of the building. He waved back in her direction. Was he really waving at her or just clearing his pipe of spittle? There was no future in it either way, she decided, and turned to look out across the countryside.

There was a giggle above her and something touched her head. She turned quickly and looked up. There was no one to be

42

seen, but a matchbox, suspended on a string, spun lazily at eye level. She caught it, and the vibrations she felt told her there was someone holding the other end. Her tentative pull was answered by a corresponding pull from above. Someone strong, she thought. To feel his strength was almost as good as having him catch her hands and pull her towards him. His male presence was at once a physical reality to her. It was the closest contact she had had with a man for a long time and it thrilled her.

'You're strong,' she whispered loudly. 'Come out till I see you.'

There was laughter above and some gentle tugs to which she responded. But no one appeared.

'Come out if you're good-looking,' Elsie sang.

'I'm a clerk in holy orders,' a voice intoned from above. 'I daren't look on the face of a woman.'

'Come on out, Arty, you ould cod,' Elsie called.

Arty's round face peered down from above, the collar of his dressing gown covering his head like a cowl. 'What is it, my child?' he asked in what he thought might be a pastoral voice. 'What sins have you committed since your last confession?'

'I committed adultery, Father,' Elsie giggled.

'By yourself – or with another?' Arty enquired gravely.

'With a fellow called Arty Byrne. He tempted me, Father.'

'Begod, Elsie, if I thought I did,' Arty crowed in his natural voice, 'I'd jump down there this minute.'

'Bring a man with you when you're coming,' Elsie teased.

'Who wants me?' Vincent leaned over and looked down into her smiling face.

'Hello, Vincent. Any new talent up there at all?'

Arty and Vincent were nice fellows, and as they would hardly ever meet in real life anyway, she felt free to say to them whatever outrageous thing came into her head – and they to her.

43

It gave an edge and excitement to existence that could not be had in any other way. It was like writing ridiculous or romantic letters – an escape into the larger world of the imagination.

Elsie stretched herself discontentedly in the evening light. 'Do you think anything exciting will ever happen to us in our lives at all, or will we always be stuck in this place?'

It was a question to which none of them had an answer. Arty and Vincent leaned with chins in cupped hands and looked down at her.

'It's not fair,' Arty said after a while. 'They say you've free will and you must save your soul by making a choice between good and evil. But what chance have we got of making any choice? I mean to say, what opportunity have the likes of us to rob a bank or kill six million people – or even commit adultery?'

'You're a dirty old man, Arty Byrne, that's what you are.' Elsie shaded her eyes and looked up at him saucily.

'I know,' Arty agreed. 'All I'm saying is that there's not much scope for dirty old men around here.'

'I wouldn't be too sure of that,' Elsie flirted. Then she was gone suddenly and they could hear a nurse's voice scolding her below.

'Elsie Hogan,' Arty mimicked as they withdrew, 'you should be in your bed.' He stuck out his tongue and blew rudely.

They sat down on Vincent's bed and stared out over the summer countryside.

'This is the kind of evening a crowd of us would get up on our bicycles and go for a spin out the country,' Vincent sighed. 'A bicycle is a great thing of a summer's evening.'

'If there's one thing I have my bellyful of, it's bicycles,' Arty said with a venom that surprised Vincent. 'The back yard at home is always full of them. The hall is stuffed tight with them – so tight you couldn't get in or out. We have new ones upstairs in the bedrooms. The walls down the stairway are hung with spare parts. There are bicycles all over the shop and the street outside – bicycles upended, frames without wheels, tyres with their guts hanging out, heaps of old chains, broken pedals, rusty handlebars, saddles stripped down to the springs. Don't talk to me about bicycles.'

'It's different when your ould fellow has a bicycle shop, I suppose,' Vincent agreed.

'Yes,' Arty grimaced, 'and there in the middle of all the mess you'll find him, the butt of a cigarette hanging from his lip, and every second, "goddamn" and "blast" out of him when the wrench slips and he tears a lump out of his finger.'

'You don't seem to like him very much,' Vincent said mildly.

'Did y' ever see him up here, did you?' Arty asked sharply.

'No, is he not well?'

'Well enough to go out to the pubs. But not well enough to throw his leg over one of his old bikes and come up here. My mother is always making excuses for him. But I know him. He just couldn't be bothered.'

'Do you handle anything besides bicycles?' Vincent asked, to divert him from the subject of his father.

'Accessories,' Arty said, 'lamps, carriers, baskets, pumps, three-speed gears, saddlebags. We sell a few musical instruments too. That's how I learned to play the accordion.'

'Give us a tune, then.' Playing was the one thing that really cheered Arty up and cheering up was what he needed in his present mood.

'My mother comes nearly every week on the bus. Couldn't he come once in a while with her?'

'My father is dead,' Vincent said.

'Was he all right – as a father, I mean?' Arty asked after a silence.

'Yes.'

Arty waited for Vincent to say more, but he kept silent.

'All right to your mother too?'

'Yes. She's never been the same since.'

'It's the wrong people die,' Arty reflected. 'The world is badly divided.' He picked up the accordion, slipped one strap over his shoulder and let his fingers ramble over the keys. 'You know, you'll laugh at this,' he said, 'but when I was about twelve, I used pretend he was only my uncle. I said to myself maybe my real father died or went away and nobody ever told me. I used walk around the town and look at men – nice pleasant men I saw in the shops or on the streets – and wonder if one of them wasn't my father. Wasn't that a daft kind of thing to do?'

Vincent smiled – a smile that had its origin in sympathy rather than amusement – and nodded wordlessly. 'My father was a guard,' he said after a while. 'He died suddenly.'

'That was tough,' Arty said, 'real tough.'

'My mother still has his uniform and all his clothes. She keeps them in a big box on top of the wardrobe.'

'The top of my mother's wardrobe is probably covered at this very minute with bicycle tubes in little boxes,' Arty said. 'God!' he continued with a studied yawn, as if regretting such intimate confidences and wishing to restore things to their proper perspective. 'It takes all kinds to make a world.' He shrugged off the accordion and stretched himself. 'Do you know what I'd really like to do with my life?'

'What?'

'I'd like to get a job in a dance band. I played a bit at weddings and parties – and for the mummers.'

'You're not going to stick to the bicycle shop, then?'

'If I had my way, I'd kick them all to hell. I wouldn't mind motorbikes, though. Did I ever tell you about the bike I was building? There was this fellow –'

'You told me,' Vincent said.

'About the fellow with the old Norton?'

'Yes.'

'You should see it, Vincent. That's what you'd call a real bike! Just let me out of here and old Byrne will be off to the the TT races in the Isle of Man. Brrrrr! Brrrrr! Can't you just hear her revving up? God! To be doing ninety on a twisting mountain road! That'd really be living!'

'More like dying!' Vincent laughed.

'Byrne the Indestructible!' Arty cried. 'Setting up a new record on every lap. Girls swooning on the dangerous bends. The high scream of engines. God! What I'd give for that kind of life!'

Sometimes now the outside world and his previous existence seemed a chimera. The only reality was the room with its apple-green walls and white, sloped ceiling. His family were intruders, insubstantial wraiths out of a dreamworld, coming and going through a mist, solid and corporeal enough while they were there, fading into tenuity when they left.

The rest was even more tenuous, more speculative. Was there a room somewhere at the top of a tall house in the city where he had lodged, a shared room, ugly with the smell of stale feet, and flabby, flowered wallpaper, and a cracked ewer sitting upright on a marble-topped table, like a surprised corpse on a mortuary slab? Had he really sat in those tiered lecture halls taking notes? Who was in that room, in those lecture halls now? Or did things cease to exist – as dreams did – when one's consciousness of them lapsed?

How had he caught this mean insidious thing? In what moment of innocent unawareness had it breached his citadel? Had it lain in wait specially for him, nurturing the secret hour? Or was it just another example of inconsequential blind chance putting its mischievous finger into the working of the divine plan? Was there a divine plan at all, or did chance rule everything?

How did one pinpoint the origin of anything, the exact moment of falling in love, of an awareness of sin? When had he first known that something serious was amiss? Certainly on that afternoon when the conviction of his own mortality came on him with a rush of bright red foam that soured his mouth and stained his handkerchief. Earlier, with those debilitating night sweats that he came to dread. Earlier still, when he looked at his emaciated face in the glass. But how easily he had explained away the lassitude, the bone-weary lethargy that sat like old age on his shoulders.

Where, or how, or when didn't matter any more; neither did why. It had happened. It was reality. It had to be coped with. It was easy now, perhaps, to trace the breakdown to that period at the end of his first year when he had gone down with pneumonia. He had been confined to bed in that top-storey garret, and had risen before he was quite recovered to take his examinations. Afterwards he had returned home to a relapse and a long convalescence in the middle of green fields, under those benign trees that had spread their protective branches over his childhood.

He wondered about trees and grass and the tumbling riches of the hedgerows, their scents and flavours, the shape and feel of growing things, the honeyed breath of life rising from the earth, curling eddies of wind, soft as feathers on the face, the long languors of a summer evening, the cooling plunge into water. He wondered what there was of value in such things that could so shape and savour the quality of a life.

He thought often of his own life, but could see no pattern or purpose in it. Had he simply been born to die before achieving anything? Was this his only function? His mind relucted against such emptiness. But when he asked himself why he should live, or what he could hope to achieve, or in what way the world would be impoverished by his premature loss, he could find no answer – no answer that wasn't self-indulgent and presumptuous. The best he could urge was that life was a precious thing, a unique thing wherever it existed, that its justification was not its usefulness but its existence, that its needless destruction, like the thoughtless trampling of a flower, diminished in some way the totality of creation and left a hiatus, however insignificant, that could never again be filled.

'No, don't write to him, child,' Mrs Doran had advised Lily, who sought comfort by confiding in her. 'It wouldn't do any good.'

'But it might,' Lily had protested. 'And it couldn't do any harm.'

'You'd be humiliating yourself – making a doormat of yourself.'

But Lily's mood had been such that she would willingly have spread herself under his feet and counted herself lucky to have him walk on her. She had written him a letter. But it was still in her locker. The fear of taking an irrevocable step had inhibited her at the last. There might be something in the letter that would alienate him entirely, something clumsily put, some presumption on her part that would divide them for ever. Better to live in vague ambiguity with the expectation – or at least the possibility – that he would turn up some day and explain that it had all been a terrible mistake.

Then, in another mood, she had taken her pen again and written him a stinging rebuke, calling him a fair-weather friend for abandoning her in her sickness, a cowardly ignoramus for subscribing to the popular ostracism of TB and its victims, a shallow good-timer, unworthy of any decent girl's love.

'That's the spirit!' Mrs Doran had said.

But Lily had kept that letter in her locker, too, and cried a great deal over it, lamenting her loneliness and the faithlessness of men.

Mrs Doran had been very kind. She had listened to her and invited her confidence. She had encouraged her to flesh out her life and in return had made revelations of her own, so that over the days they grew together in understanding and sympathy. She was a slight, patient, little woman with a history of misfortune. Two sons and a daughter had already passed this way before her, and she had seen their funerals go to the graveyard inside eighteen months of each other. None of them had been over twenty. She had been inside herself when John, the eldest, was taken. She had watched from her bed as his funeral went down the avenue. There were only her husband and the youngest left, Mary, a girl of ten. She lived in dread of either of them catching the scourge.

Lily liked Mr Doran. He was a tall stooped man with a lined face and kind eyes. He stepped awkwardly across the polished floor like a horse on ice and sat quietly beside his wife's bed all through visiting time, his head inclined slightly towards her as she talked. She had never seen them holding hands or kissing or exchanging any token of affection, but as she watched them over the weeks, she had the conviction that some unbreakable bond held them together. She noticed that, unlike other men, he came regularly, always stayed the full time, was never in a hurry to go. She noticed particularly that they talked a great deal. She always felt that for both of them, in spite of their tragic loss, a fire still burned on the hearth and warmed them with its glow.

In the evenings Lily lay in bed and watched her friend Elsie and some of the other young women flirting on the verandah. She liked Elsie for her vitality and her optimism – even if she could not share it. Elsie was a bright light in the gloom. Her laugh mocked the tragedy around. It might be foolhardy, rooted in barren clay, but it had courage – and courage was something to be admired. 'We might as well have a laugh while we're in it,' was Elsie's motto. 'We'll be dead long enough.'

Yes, but most of us will be dead before we have ever really lived, Lily thought, and there's not much to laugh about in that. Even if we do live, what kind of half life will it be, with the stigma of shame on us, and all our friends – or those we thought our friends – turning their backs on us.

'There's a fellow out here asking for you,' Elsie shouted in. 'Says he met you when you were up for your collapse. He wants to know how you are.'

Lily smiled vaguely but did not answer.

Elsie bounded in and sat on the bed. 'Shake out of it, Lily. Vincent is a very nice fellow.'

'I know,' Lily said, remembering his words of encouragement outside the treatment room. 'Tell him I'm all right.'

'Will I tell him you're mad about him?' Elsie asked, her eyes shining with mischief.

'Don't say anything of the sort!' Lily said in alarm. 'Why would you tell him a lie like that?'

'It's only a bit of fun,' Elsie laughed.

'Don't, Elsie, please. Tell him whatever you like about yourself, but leave me out of it.'

'I'll tell him you're asking for him, anyway. There's no harm in that.' She leaped up and headed for the verandah again.

Lily turned away and picked up a magazine from her locker. She leafed through the pages until she became aware that Elsie had returned and was standing there, looking at her and smiling.

'This is getting to be quite a romance,' Elsie laughed. 'He wants to know if you'll write to him.'

She stood there, smiling and waiting. Then her face slowly broke into dismay, incomprehension and alarm when Lily buried her head in the magazine and started to cry.

'What is it?' Elsie enquired solicitously. 'Did I say something wrong?' Lily was the strangest girl sometimes. It was impossible to understand her.

Though he was a letter writer of distinction, as most of the girls
with whom he had corresponded would have testified, there
was one letter whose composition did not come easy to Vincent
Finn. This was his weekly letter to his mother who lived in a little
terraced house in town, where he and his elder brother Peter had
grown up, and where they had all been happy and cosy together
until his father died.

Looking back on his father's death now, it seemed to Vincent
that he had taken the door and rooftree with him and left them
exposed to winter's rough excesses. Whenever he thought of his
father, he saw him with the eye of childhood in that blue uniform
and shining peaked cap, which gave him some of the moral authority of God, adjusting his belt before stepping out on the street
to wrap his official presence protectively about the town. He had
collapsed one morning in the day room and was dead by the time
they got him to hospital.

What was there to say to his mother that would bring comfort
to that silent house? Tell her he was well and not to fret because
he would be home soon? Peter had come from Dublin for the
funeral, bringing his young wife with him. He was stationed in
one of the suburban barracks. They had been so proud of him

when he had gone off to join the force. There was Peter's photograph beside his father's on the mantelpiece, Peter razor sharp at the passing-out parade. Soon after had come his marriage and the birth of his first child. That left Vincent and his mother in a cold house of mourning – he quite defeated by her cancerous sorrow.

The day of his father's death had been Vincent's last day in secondary school. In spite of his mother's pleading that he should complete his year and sit for his Leaving Certificate, he had insisted on pulling about his frail shoulders the mantle of his father and had taken a job in the despatch department of a light-engineering factory in the town.

He looked gloomily across to where Arty sat, propped up like himself with a writing pad on his knees. Things were going well with Arty. His pen ran fluently along the page. His protruding tongue and smirk of self-complacency were enough to indicate that he was writing to a girl and that the fiction was flowing freely. There was an air of excitement about him, as if he had scented inspiration on the wing and was hot in pursuit to bag it in a net of words before it could escape.

What Vincent could not know – even when Arty, looking up suddenly and catching his eye, smiled broadly and beckoned him over – was that he had been witnessing a breakthrough into more daring fictional modes. He smiled rather bleakly back, reflecting the sombreness of his thoughts. But Arty, dropping his pad and clenching both fists at ear level, like a footballer who has scored a goal, grinned widely and called, 'I've something to show you. Jeez, Vincent, I've thought of a great wheeze!'

With relief Vincent laid aside the limping, half-completed letter to his mother and sprang out of bed.

'Listen!' Arty was saying. 'Listen!' He took up his writing pad,

54

licking his lips in anticipation, like a child about to indulge himself in ice cream. '"Dear Janice – "'

'Who's Janice?' Vincent asked without much enthusiasm.

'A new one. A new one,' Arty bubbled. 'I'm making a clean sweep and scrapping the old crowd. They'd put years on you. From now on I'm going to live more dangerously.' He pointed to a magazine lying beside him. 'I got her in there. And I got the idea there too. "Fond of adventure" it says. Well, I'm going to give her all the adventure she can take. Listen to this.'

Vincent smiled. Arty's enthusiasm was beginning to work its magic on him. You could always depend on Arty for some distracting game that would sidestep reality and get you through the day.

Dear Janice,

I'd just returned from climbing the Matterhorn, when I came across this magazine where you advertise for a pen friend who likes adventure. That about describes me all right. When I'm not hanging by the fingernails off mountains, or schooling a horse over Beecher's, I'm probably cutting my way with a machete through the Amazonian jungle in search of some lost civilisation, or exploring the polar icecap ...

He looked up to see how Vincent was reacting.

'Bloody good!' Vincent said. Then, recognising the sheer fantasy of it, he added, 'You don't think you're laying it on a bit thick?'

'She said she wanted adventure, didn't she?' Arty was full of the madness of it.

'Try it anyway.'

'There's no fun in the yokes we're writing to,' Arty said. 'There's no more romance in them than in a bag of prunes. The beauty of this wheeze is that there's no need to be yourself any more. I can be anybody I like. Who in her sound mind would want to write to a crock with the Con, anyway!'

It was unfortunate for Arty's scheme that Janice proved a dud. Her sense of adventure, or her sense of humour, or both, were obviously inadequate. After a week of high expectancy a curt note arrived.

Dear Arty Byrne,

I don't write to loonies.

Yours sincerely,
Janice Jenkins

But there were others who were gullible enough, or sporting enough, to continue the correspondence, and Arty embarked on dashing careers as racing driver, band leader, football star. There was never any mention of his illness and he was always carefully ambiguous about his address. Ardeevan was his country seat, or a luxury hotel, but never a hospital – except on one mad occasion when a spate of letters began to arrive for Mr Arthur D. ('for Damn-all, but it will impress her') Byrne, FRCSI, the eminent surgeon.

His father and Michael were busy at the hay, but it was such a fine day that Liam and herself had decided to cycle the fifteen miles, Eileen told him. Where was Liam? He knew he had been worried about Liam – had gone through a phase where he imagined he was dead and no one would tell him. Eileen laughed. Liam was outside, but they wouldn't let him in. He was only thirteen and children were not allowed to visit the wards.

Eileen was flushed after her journey, a little breathless as she sat there. Her wrists, resting in her lap, seemed to him to be long, bony. The blue veins under the pale skin gave her a delicate, vulnerable appearance.

It was pleasant to have just one visitor. Sometimes, especially in the early days, when they had all crowded around him, he had become heated and uncomfortable – and eventually confused – and wished for the visitors' bell to ring so that he could have a little more air and throw down the blankets and lie there with his eyes closed, cooling off, not thinking of anything at all.

'You look a little better,' Eileen said.

'I've stopped losing weight,' he told her. 'I've even put on a pound.'

'That's great!' Eileen turned towards him with that eager, shining look of hers. 'They'll all be delighted to hear that.'

She looked thin. The delicate line of her cheekbones seemed more pronounced than he had known it and her high colour after the cycling had given her a fevered look. It was a habit of his, since his illness, to look closely at people for signs of sickness and decay. He had become obsessed with mortality.

Eileen's simple faith that he was improving was an illusion. The disease was like that. There were dramatic improvements – though nothing dramatic had happened to him yet – and there were slow relapses. It was a cunning disease, sometimes devouring rabidly and sometimes hibernating in the flesh for years before sweeping like a humid fire through the tissues.

He was able to sit up for short periods now and showed an interest in reading again. But holding a book for any length of time heated and weakened him and he soon had to put it aside and lie flat. Sometimes he drifted into a light sleep. More often he lapsed into long reveries, peopled by slow-moving shadows out of his past, the faces of his childhood, snatches of conversation endlessly repeated, the unfolding of a road leading along the devious routes of past experience to the distant present. He would dwell interminably on the beating of hailstones on the corrugated iron roof of an outhouse where he had been isolated once in childhood during a sudden thunderstorm. The exact form and flavour of his fear soured his memory like the taste of vomit as he huddled there awaiting rescue, the lightning penetrating his closed eyes and the thunder rolling and cracking, until the world seemed to be riven apart and crashing in ruins about him. Then, the stinging rattle of hail, softening to sleet, through which he ran, crouching, across the whitened yard to safety.

'They came and fumigated your room,' Eileen said. 'They told us to gather up all your clothes and things and burn them outside. Then they closed the windows and sealed them and lit a sulphur candle in the room and locked and sealed the door and told us not to open it again for forty-eight hours.'

'It's very infectious,' he said. 'That's one of the most dangerous things about it.'

'They want us all to go for x-ray,' Eileen said. 'Doctor O'Driscoll gave us a note to take with us. He gave us a long speech about it being our duty, but we can't get Daddy to go and Michael isn't very keen either. We'll have to some day, won't we? But nobody wants to think about it or talk about it with you here – and everything.'

The thought that he might have infected one of them troubled him after she had gone. He remembered his premonitions about Liam, whose room he had shared when he was on holidays. A young person of Liam's age was very vulnerable.

On Monday afternoons, Jim Kielthy, a morose, melancholy, heron of a man, lifting his bony shanks carefully, as if he were wading through dangerous shallows, pushed a trolley of books from ward to ward and distributed them. Earlier in the day he had gone about with a typewritten list, frayed and illegible from many foldings, and a notebook in which he had written – with the stub of a puce pencil that he had parked behind his ear – the names of the patients and the books they requested.

Jim was an odd librarian, who got no pleasure from books. He never read one and knew nothing of them beyond the titles. It was a job he had been asked to do and he did it. In the morning he went about, licking his pencil patiently, while he waited for someone to make up his mind.

'What's this one like, Jim?'

Jim would wade over carefully and bend his long neck to peruse the list. 'Well, now, I can't rightly say,' he would begin with immeasurable gravity, 'but I hear good reports of it.'

There were only two kinds of books that Jim was aware of – ones of which he had heard either good or bad reports. He never bothered to reveal the source of these reports, but the solemnity with which he delivered judgement lent authority to his utterance. In the afternoon he distributed the books like a farmer flinging turnips to cattle.

Phil Turner was no great reader either. But he liked illustrated magazines with photographs of boxers and athletes, or weightlifters and body-builders, and lately – having leafed through some books he saw on Frank O'Shea's locker – he had become interested in art and Greek mythology, and waited patiently on Monday afternoons for the sound of Jim's trolley squeaking through the wards.

'Boys o' boys!' Jim eyed him oddly. 'I don't know why you spend so much of your time looking at naked statues.'

'Look at that, now.' Phil laid his moist finger on the thigh of a graceful Greek youth. 'Isn't that a work of art, all the same?'

Jim bent to look; then, his interest in naked youths quickly waning, he drew a grubby piece of newspaper from his pocket and unfolded it. 'Hey! It might match you better to look at this. Read it and tell me what you think of it.'

Phil took the torn square of paper and looked at it. He read it through carefully, his eyes brightening as they followed the print.

'Would it be worth a try?' Jim asked.

'Worth a try! This is the best news yet,' Phil said. 'We'll send for some. Are you on?'

'It says one pound a bottle. Wouldn't that be a lot?'

'But look what it says here! Look what it can do!' Phil rubbed his lips with the back of his hand and read aloud in a curiously childish voice, stumbling over the difficult words.

C U R E   G U A R A N T E E D !

Do you suffer from
TUBERCULOSIS, EMPHYSEMA, BRONCHITIS,
or other respiratory diseases?
INSTANT CURE GUARANTEED
to users of my
HERBAL ELIXIR

Write for a bottle today (enclosing £1) to:
HARRY DAGG, 426 BLENHEIM STREET, BELFAST

'It's too good a chance to miss,' he said.

'Will we try it?' Jim asked.

'Sure, we'll try it!'

'Ten bob a man, what do you say?'

'Done.'

'You write the letter,' Jim said. 'I'll be back with the money as soon as I get rid of these.'

He seized the trolley and pushed off, his scraggy neck and beaked face preceding him, a flush of anticipation burning the cheekbones. At the door something occurred to him and he came back to whisper. 'Not a word about this to anyone. We might make a fortune out of it yet. What's to stop us from getting a

60

crateful – if it's good – and selling it for thirty bob a bottle? Thirty bob isn't much to get rid of a thing like the Con, is it?'

'Or two pounds, for that matter!' Phil said.

Every three months, if they were fit for the journey, patients could expect to be sent to the county hospital for x-ray. The ambulance would call for them in the afternoon, and they would be taken the twenty-odd miles there and back.

Sometimes, if the company was right and Marty, the ambulance man, agreeable, and the nurse who sat beside him not dissenting, a hurried stop was made at a wayside pub and the men would troop in to stand at the bar and down a few bottles of stout and pretend for a while that they were free and presently – just like the odd local they might find there, placidly filling his pipe – would walk out into the light and go their separate ways.

The journey had an unsettling effect on some. It was not unknown for these patients to mope about for a day or two after their return, then hurriedly call for their cases, throw their few belongings into them, discharge themselves against all prudent advice and hurry down the avenue, a determined set to their heads – and the foul, fatal disease ticking away like a time bomb inside them.

For others it was a preliminary to change. If they were lucky, it meant a step nearer the door. It might also mean a new course of treatment or being sent to a larger sanatorium for surgery – anything from thoracoplasty to pneumonectomy.

For Frank O'Shea the choice became one – as he put it in his own sardonic way – between butchery or burial.

'Thoracoplasty is your best hope,' said Doctor Staples, who had taken him down to his office to break it to him gently.

'You mean my only hope, don't you?' Frank asked sharply.

'In the long run – yes,' answered Doctor Staples, who was an honest man. He pointed to the illuminated x-ray. 'You see how your right lung shows wide cavitation?' He touched the x-ray with a pointer. 'Here and here and here?'

'If you say so …'

'It hasn't responded to treatment. There is little sign of calcification of the lesions. This one is so large that it never would calcify anyhow. On the other hand, your left lung, here, is in pretty good shape. Now, our best – our only – hope of saving it is to collapse the right one permanently. As long as it remains the way it is, it will be a source of infection for your good lung. You understand a little of the operation, I suppose?'

'Scientifically or emotionally?' Frank enquired.

'What do you mean?'

'For a doctor like you,' Frank said, 'there's only the scientific, isn't there? A patient's ribs are removed. The flesh falls in on the lung and it collapses. The patient lives or dies. If he lives, he is partly deformed or badly deformed.'

'There's no need whatsoever to be deformed,' Doctor Staples said, his composure ruffled. 'There are exercises to deal with that. You'll have a physiotherapist to help you. There is no danger whatever of scoliosis, if the prescribed exercises are adhered to.'

'If …' Frank said sarcastically. 'It's a pretty large "if". Some of us remember Doctor Langan. He did a three months' spell of duty here last autumn.'

'Yes, I remember him.'

'Lopsided Langan they used to call him. He had a thora, hadn't he? And he was a doctor!'

'There are two things to be said about Doctor Langan,' Doctor Staples said very deliberately. 'The first is that doctors don't necessarily make good patients. The second, and this, I think, is the only important one as far as you're concerned, the second is

62

that he survived. He has returned to work. Remember, it must be six years since he had his operation. Think about that, now.'

'Fair enough,' Frank conceded. 'Now we come to the emotional bit. Emotionally this thora thing is the Big Bang. It calls for heroism and I'm no hero.'

'You're an educated man,' the doctor said.

'I'm a man,' Frank told him. 'When it comes to things like this, there are only men and women. You can't educate against fear and pain. In some ways the educated man, the imaginative man – because of his knowledge or imagination – is more susceptible than others. How would you, with all your medical understanding of what is involved, like to have a thora?'

'Fortunately,' Doctor Staples said in an apologetic tone, 'I don't have to make the decision. But I concede your point.'

'What are my chances?' Frank asked suddenly.

'Much better than, say, Doctor Langan's were in his day.'

'How many ribs?'

'It will have to be a full thoracoplasty, I'm afraid. It would be done in two stages. Half the ribs would be removed first and the rest a fortnight or so later.'

'With its support gone, what's to keep the right side from keeling over? Isn't it the same as taking away the front and gable wall from a house and expecting the roof to stand?'

'That's where physiotherapy comes in. The postoperative physiotherapy is crucial. Once you recognise that fact, and accept it, and follow the regime of exercises scrupulously, there is nothing to worry about.' He looked at Frank, waiting for a response. 'Well, what do you say?'

'I'll – think about it,' Frank said.

'Discuss it with Mrs O'Shea, won't you?'

'Yes. I'll discuss it.'

Kitty O'Shea wasn't a great one for discussion. If it has to be done, it has to be done, would be her tack. But it's up to yourself. Nobody else can make the decision. Then she would go back to toss that dangerous red head of hers (tinted now, of course) behind the bar, flashing her indiscreet smile at customers – ingratiating commercial travellers like prowling tomcats, randy youngsters, their milk teeth awash in their first pint.

It had seemed a good alliance at the time – Kitty, the attractive young widow, with her comfortable bar and grocery, and himself, the impecunious teacher, new to the village, the training college a few short years behind him, fond of his comfort, hungry for a security he had never known – hungry, most of all, for the rich pastures of the flesh into which she had invited him. All that first spring and summer – even yet – was suffused in a hot glow, a lethargic dream of grace into which he had slipped with the same ease as he had slipped through the window she had nightly left unlatched for him to the fulfilment of her bed.

It had seemed to him ever since that those clandestine couplings had been more of a real marriage than anything that came afterwards. It was as if there was something in her nature that craved the secretive and the illicit for the release of passion. Perhaps if there had been children, things might have been different.

Her first husband had died in a cliff accident on their honeymoon and Frank sometimes wondered whether she wasn't taking it out on him for that ultimate betrayal.

6

Arty's fantasy life was beginning to create problems. The trouble started when a girl called Madeleine – a singularly foolish and gullible young woman, obsessed with fame and thrilled by Arty's outrageous adventures – wrote to say that she was coming to visit him. At first he was not too worried, because with Vincent's help, he had already devised a plan to meet just such an eventuality.

'It's curtains for Madeleine, I'm afraid,' Vincent said, reaching for his pen.

'I'm sorry to lose her,' Arty rubbed his eyes in mock tragedy. 'I'll never find the likes of her again. She'd believe anything.'

'Let's hope she'll believe this!' Vincent had found his writing pad and began to compose:

Dear FOOLISH young lady,

A word in your ear. It has come to my attention that you are in amorous correspondence with that WICKED DECEIVER Arty Byrne. Did you know that he is tied to ANOTHER? He is the FATHER OF THREE YOUNG CHILDREN – not to mention TWO MORE by his LAWFUL WIFE. A nod is as good as a wink.

From a FRIEND

'That should settle Madeleine!' Arty laughed.

But it didn't. By return of post came a letter assuring him of her undying esteem, and repeating her intention of visiting him in spite of the scurrilous note (which she was enclosing in the hope that he might recognise the handwriting), obviously composed by someone who was jealous of their intimacy and had a mind like a sewer. She didn't care in the least whether it was true or not. He had every right to be a father if he wanted to. She couldn't think of a better father and wouldn't mind having him as a father for her own children – inside or outside wedlock – should he so desire. She understood perfectly that adventurous men, sporting men, famous men should sow a few wild oats and not be held too much in check by the strict rein of morality.

'This one is a right loony!' Arty said, when he had got over the first shock.

'Or she's pulling your leg,' Vincent suggested. 'Maybe she was pulling your leg all the time and you never knew it.'

'She hasn't the brains,' Arty scoffed.

'Do you think you're the only one with brains?'

Arty fingered his scalp with more than usual desperation. 'You're not really serious about her pulling my leg, are you?'

Vincent shrugged. 'I suppose not. Judging by her other letters she wouldn't have the wit.'

'What'll we do now?'

'Write her another letter.'

But it was easier said than done. Several days went by and much ink was spilt before something clicked and they struck the right creative mood. They laughed a great deal as they composed, congratulating each other on their cleverness, expressing the wish that they could be there to see her face when she opened it.

Dear Madam,

We have been instructed by our client, Mr Ernest Byrne, to advise you that your unscrupulous designs on the affection of his only son, Mr Arthur Byrne, will be resisted by him to the full extent of the law.

This is not the first occasion on which he has had to intervene to protect the heir of his vast business interests from the grasp of an unprincipled adventuress. Mr Arthur, unfortunately, is of a trusting disposition and is, therefore, an easy prey to such as you.

We advise you, accordingly, to lay off. No further letter of yours will be delivered to him, but will be kept as evidence and used against you in a court of law.

Mr Arthur, in any case, is no longer available at his usual address, being at this very moment aboard the SS *Adventure* on an extended Caribbean cruise.

We also beg to advise you that it is his father's intention to arrange a marriage for him – which will take place shortly in Caracas – to the daughter of the Venezuelan oil millionaire Señor Vincenzo de Finno.

Yours sincerely,
Kielthy & Turner, Solicitors

Sometimes Commander Barnwell, who took the law into his own hands and ignored rest hours, came to sit beside him and talk – of Clover Lodge and the countryside, of politics ('that damned charlatan, de Valera, and his policy of neutrality – no sense of loyalty or gratitude to the hand that fed him ...'), of the lamentable climate and, most of all, of the First World War. He had been a young sub-lieutenant on Jellicoe's flagship, the *Iron Duke*, and had seen his first action at the Battle of Jutland.

'Between the cursed mist and smoke,' he said, 'you couldn't see your hand. Nothing but the flash of guns. The only time you

67

saw another vessel was when there was a direct hit and one exploded. I saw the *Invincible* go up – pieces of armour plating, as big as a two-storey house, tossed aloft. There were only six survivors out of a crew of over a thousand. Ah, but von Scheer, the fox, had all the luck! Slipped through us in the mist and away.'

The Commander brought him magazines, *Field & Stream*, and *Country Life*, which he particularly loved to leaf through. It had the very breath and flavour of the countryside – even if it was only the English countryside. The eye rested gratefully on superb photographs of ancient and gracious houses, lych gates, Dutch barns, Dorset barrows, cool country lanes, the winding contours of a dry-stone wall. The leisured articles were a joy to read, full of rich country wisdom, restful, loving, calm, quarried from that marvellous vein of contemplative rural prose beginning with Walton and continuing through Gilbert White's *Selborne* to the novels of Hardy and beyond.

Of late the Commander rarely sat for more than a few minutes at a time. He preferred to stroll about the room with his hand on his abdomen.

'It's this damned air thing,' he protested. 'Most uncomfortable when you sit. Pushes everything up. You feel it here in the shoulders. Cramps the stomach too. Feel it when you try to eat. Feeling of nausea – disgusting! They stick a damned great needle down here, sou'west of the belly button and pump you up like a bloody football. Wouldn't stand for it myself. Don't believe in it. But Mildred – the old girl, you know – thought it would be a good idea. Must humour them, dammit. That's all we men are good for, what!' He laughed a soft, phlegm-strangled laugh that changed into a prolonged cough and turned suddenly where he stood and went back to his room. The metal lid of a sputum mug snapped back and he hawked chokingly into it.

'God!' he muttered aloud when he had finished. 'Why wasn't I taken at sea where a man could face his end with dignity!'

Hearing the brisk tap of Sister Cooney's heels on the corridor, he slipped into bed and lay there, his breathing rapid and his colour heightened after the exertion.

Sister Cooney looked in and smiled. 'Everything all right, Commander?'

'Yes, yes, it's just this damned cough,' he gasped irritably.

'I'll get you something for it. I'll send it down to you.'

She crossed the corridor to the other room. Her mottled skin whitened as she smiled. 'I've good news for you. You're off the bedpan routine. We'll have a commode brought in for you tomorrow, and after a week or so, when you've found your legs, you'll be able to go to the bathroom down the corridor. And, oh,' she thumbed through a bundle of letters she held in her hand, 'there's this for you.' She put a letter on the trolley that straddled the bed, smiled again in her raddled courtesan's way and went out.

He recognised the handwriting easily enough. He reached for the letter with a sigh. There was something he had to do, something he should have done already, something he thought of doing every time a letter from her arrived.

She was a gentle girl whom he had met at a party. He might even be in love with her if he were to look deep enough into himself. But love, in his changed circumstances, was only a self-indulgent luxury. There was no good reason for involving her in sickness and misery. The one thing he could do for her that would not be clinging and weak was to untie whatever emotional strands held them together and set her free. She would resent her freedom for a while, but later could contemplate it without guilt. That was the one parting gift he could give her.

They had walked a lot and talked and drank coffee in strange and unfrequented cafés around the city. They had laughed and run and done silly, innocent things – trees and houses and telegraph poles and running water had a newborn look, as if they were seeing them for the first time. Their reflections in a pool of oily water was a matter of wonder, with the slow-moving clouds uncoiling behind their heads and the sinuous, blue-green ooze, edged with purple, of their laughing faces. It was a shared warmth of experience that was a revelation to him, wrapping that late autumn and winter in a haze of coloured light like the prismatic sky over the manifold, mysterious city.

Breaking it off would be a kind of death – a death without consolation or comfort, apart from the bleak knowledge that it was for her own good and had to be done.

Lily lay back on her high pillows and thought of the drapery shop where she had worked. Someone else was in her place now, and Maureen and Ellen and the new girl would laugh and exchange confidences and there would be no place for her in their thoughts and conversation at all. When she thought of the shop – or of most other things in her life – she soon became melancholy and cried. Tears lay like a great fathomless ocean beneath the surface of her world. She had only to break through a thin crust to be engulfed.

Like her home and Joe, the shop had been part of her identity. It defined and authenticated her. Here she was no more than a floating piece of wreckage or a fluff of thistledown blown about at the mercy of an arbitrary wind. Behind the counter she was a real person, competent, assured. 'Miss Moore will look after you.' The manager Mr Hayes would smile in her direction and she would smile back and nod to the customer. 'Can I help you, madam?' When the sale had been made, and the parcel wrapped neatly and tied, and the docket issued, and the satisfied customer steered towards the till, behind which Mr Hayes hovered, there was the feeling of a job well done.

She loved the smell of new cloth, its individual feel and colour – the warmth of wool, the crispness of cotton, the smooth, cool whisper of silk. She loved the brashness of clashing bolts of material on a shelf, the ordered secrecy of boxes with their cabalistic price markings into which she had been initiated, the counter spread with garments after a sale. She loved to examine the new stock coming in, to select something fashionable and have Mr Hayes set it aside for her until she had paid for it by weekly deductions from her wages.

Mr Hayes, a dapper little man in a pinstripe suit, was decent like that, though Maureen – who was a lively one and not above teasing – maintained that he often made them reach for boxes on high shelves for no good reason except that it gave him an opportunity to stare at their legs. She was inclined to hint also, with her insinuating giggle, that he showed more than a professional interest in the lingerie counter.

Lily wept for the scored counters with their brass measuring rules, for the huge scissors on a cord which she liked to wear occasionally around her neck because it gave her that professional feeling. She wept for the ever-opening door and the varied, verbose clientele. She wept, because her illness had diminished her.

From where she lay, she could see out over the summer countryside. Below her, the river unwound lazily like the coils of a life linking mystery to mystery. She felt oppressed by the overwhelming statement of green. Her environment had always been the winding intimacy of streets, the whispered security of terraced houses and the civil code of asphalt and concrete.

Vincent was from the town too – not her own town, but another similar town, with similar early-morning smells of lighting fires and fresh bread and acrid gutters and petrol fumes and damp walls. She knew that much about him, because in spite of her refusal to engage in light-hearted correspondence, he had continued to enquire after her, to send messages through Elsie – messages to which she replied perfunctorily – and eventually to write.

Though she was moved in some way by his letter, she neither felt obliged nor disposed to respond, until Elsie threatened to write on her behalf, urging that it was a shame to lose such a nice fellow to some girl in another ward – and that it was as sinful as a starving woman passing up good food, when they were all famished for a bit of romance, even if it was only at one or two removes. Lily didn't really think that Elsie – giddy though she was – would carry out her threat. But her teasing kept Vincent before Lily's mind and she found herself wondering about his motives. She wondered, too, if his feelings might be hurt and if he didn't, at least, deserve a courteous reply, even if it had to be a negative one.

The note – it was scarcely more – merely stated that she thanked him for his letter but did not feel able to write, because there was nothing to write about. She was not the sort of person who could dash off amusing letters that could be passed about from one to the other and laughed over to ease the boredom of an idle moment.

Hetty, the wardsmaid, whom she could trust to keep a secret, took the letter upstairs. Later in the day she returned with another letter from Vincent, slipping it to Lily unobserved in a bundle of clean laundry. Vincent wanted her to understand that it had never been his intention to show her letters to anyone else. He was tired of that kind of meaningless letter writing. What he had in mind was something different entirely. If they had met somewhere outside – at a dance or party – they might have sat and talked. He would have told her something about his life and she might have told him about hers and they might have passed a few pleasant minutes and, maybe, met again, if both had thought the conversation worth continuing. That was the kind of letter writing he had in mind – a sort of casual conversation about anything and everything.

His letter deserved a reply. And so the correspondence continued, a tentative revelation of self, tedious to linger over, but fascinating to themselves (especially in retrospect) as the opening of a play, where their personalities emerged from the shadows and circled warily, creating flesh and blood and forging character from words on a page.

7

In the early morning, before seven, the night nurse came, humming loudly and banging trolleys about. She carried a kidney dish with some cotton wool on it and a jar of white disinfectant out of which stuck the tops of four thermometers. She cleaned them with cotton wool and slipped them into sleepy mouths, then grabbed languid wrists and checked the pulse, making bright and alert conversation, now that her day was coming to an end, not at all disconcerted by the fact that her brightness cast a harsh glare at such an hour.

Shortly after, she returned with steaming basins for bed patients and pulled and bullied them until they sat up and washed. Later, she came again to empty the basins, to fold and hang towels on the bars behind lockers, to rearrange the blankets and tidy up before breakfast.

Frank sat drooping on the edge of his bed, a foul taste in his mouth, and fished about with blind fingers for his slippers. It was chilly at that hour with the morning mist sweeping in through the open doors across the verandah. He shrugged himself into his dressing gown, felt in his locker for his shaving gear, slung his towel across his shoulder and shuffled out to the bathroom.

He watched with curious detachment the razor shaving the strange face in the mirror. He noticed the lined cheeks, the puffed eyes, the unlovely hairs protruding from the nostrils. Vaguely in his mind stirred the remembrance of a Yeats line about the heart being fastened to a dying animal.

Back in the ward it was not unpleasant to sit wrapped in blankets and look out over the wakening fields, grey with dew, down towards the trees and the river, and see the hedges meshed with cobwebs, as manifold and intricate as the threads that linked human lives. Cattle, their hair curled and damp, their breath vaporising ahead of them, moved sluggishly, leaving green trails. A fresh earthy smell came on the raw air, a distillation of odours from humid soil and the burrowing roots of growing things. Mixed through it all was the resinous essence of trees. The sky was still indecisive, like a housewife flopping about in faded dressing gown and slippers, with insufficient energy as yet to give her mind seriously to her wardrobe for the day.

Presently came a squeak and rattle of breakfast trolleys butting through the wards. Indifferent porridge without salt or savour. Listless essays at conversation, provoking no response – like stones dropped into a bottomless well. Long stares at nothing, the mind refusing to engage in rational thought, unwilling to dredge itself upwards from the intuitive borderland of sleep.

He found himself counting drops along the railing and watching with fascination and a sense of the inevitability of things as a drop fattened and fell. He watched the next build-up and tried to anticipate the exact moment when the balance between its weight and adhesive power would be upset – never getting it quite right, always taken by surprise at the suddenness or sluggishness of its departure. He pondered idly about the experiment that might be conducted if he had a stopwatch and timed them. He wondered if it would support the theory he vaguely felt about the multiplicity and variety, and inventiveness – if that were the right word – of nature, that no two raindrops – no two of anything – were ever quite the same, that every drop was unique, as he himself was unique.

He ate without zest, without urgency – good food nullified into tastelessness by his melancholy. It seemed to him that eating had no purpose there. Nothing had any purpose. Each day fell stillborn out of the womb of night and one could do no more than observe its obsequies. There was no challenge in the light – except the challenge to survive – no morning going forth and evening return, no family to scramble for, no redeeming sacrifice to make, nothing but the turning in on self in ever-lessening circles, like a snake consuming its own tail and choking on the superfluity.

He sat, propped in pillows, and listened himself into an awareness of time and the present moment screaming back into the slipstream of the wheeling earth, irretrievably lost in the universal void. He wondered about God and the riddle of existence, and finding no answer, returned to the immediate problem, humiliating in its ordinariness, but equally baffling – how to rearrange the pillows, to relieve the pressure on his spine, to rid the bed of crumbs.

Kitty O'Shea! There was irony in the name, he had long thought. But that Kitty had been loyal to one man, at least.

'You'd better fix up your affairs,' she had said, when he told her. 'To be on the safe side,' she had added when he made no response.

'Survivor takes all,' he had smiled cynically, 'so what's the need?'

'You'll probably bury the lot of us,' she had said defensively.

Then, because he knew it would annoy her, he had said, 'I

76

don't want to be buried. I want my body to go to a hospital – a teaching hospital.'

'You can't do that!'

'Why not! Are you afraid they'd say you sold your husband's body?'

'Don't be so cynical about everything.'

'After all, you sold your own.'

'You must be out of your mind. I never did!'

'No,' he had replied angrily, 'I suppose not. You gave it for nothing – to every Tom, Dick and Harry.'

'What right have you to say that?' she had flared then. 'If only you'd been any good …'

They had been through it all many times before. What right had he to blame her, to deplore her insobriety, her venality? It was he who had been the meretricious one. Hadn't he sold himself for ease and security a long time ago? She had merely spilled herself like an open flagon and asked only to be consumed. What had he ever had to offer that could compete with the casual excitement and tongue-loosened lickerishness of a public bar?

The troubles of Arty Byrne were deepening. Madeleine had written again, telling him that she had got the strangest letter but didn't believe a word of it. Someone was pulling her leg or pulling both their legs. She would tell him all about it when she came to see him. She would be getting her holidays in August and would call on him then. She was looking forward to it impatiently.

'There's only one thing for it.' Arty massaged his skull in agitation and appealed to Vincent who sat in bed, dangling the letter between his fingers and doing his best to appear solemn. 'We'll have to end it, once and for all.'

'God, no!' Vincent leaped out in mock alarm to place himself between Arty and the balcony. 'You wouldn't throw yourself over!'

'It's serious, boy,' Arty moaned. 'You'll have to get on the pen again.'

'I know what we'll do,' Vincent said. 'We'll get out the black-bordered notepaper and do the job right.'

'That's what I meant,' Arty said.

So in the next post a letter went out to Miss Madeleine O'Reilly.

My Dear Madeleine,

It is my sad duty to inform you that your beloved Arthur was hurled into eternity in the blazing wreckage of his racing car in the Phoenix Park the other day. He died – as he had lived – without recovering consciousness. The remains were buried at sea.

This correspondence must now close.

For the next of kin,
Vincent Barrymore Finn

His first walk was to the window. It was a dormer window set chest high. He looked down over red, mossed tiles to the terrace and the walled gardens. It was the first time he had seen anything but sky since his arrival. All the greens were deeper now, fat and shiny with summer, the beech leaves dark as the face of a scolding gypsy. He looked at everything with surprise and wonder, struck suddenly with the length of his confinement. His memory, like a run-down clock stopped at spring, was still full of delicate tints and veined transparencies, unfolding like butterflies from the chrysalis. It was a shock to walk so dramatically into the brazen beat of midsummer.

There was no strength in his legs. He swayed in an uncertain line back to the bed and sat down. Then he was up again, struggling into his dressing gown. To steady himself he held on to the door as he went out. It was an effort to lift his feet up the single step to the corridor. Beside him, the carved oak banisters descended in a graceful curve. He leaned against them, breathless but triumphant. Warm kitchen smells came to him up the stairwell. Someone got into the lift below and the iron gates clanged. The floor vibrated as the lift began to move.

He launched off again up the corridor, keeping close to the wall, one hand sliding over it to steady himself. By a window he stood and looked down at the ground between the buildings. An iron fire escape (red perforated plates shining) linked both floors to the ground. Through a gap of light a crow flew with a crust in its beak. Something in its free unfettered flight shadowed his elation.

By the time he reached the lavatory he was exhausted, and had to sit down to urinate. Feeling strength coming back to him, he sat until there was a pawing at the door and it was pushed in. He sprang to close it, but before he could, a bald head came thrusting through with bulging eyes and wet, purple lips. He clutched the dressing gown round him and saw the insidious eyes follow the motion of his hand.

'Are you all right?' The throaty voice was soft as the oozing of snails.

'Yes, yes! I forgot to lock the door.' He pushed until it seemed the huge head would be crushed against the jamb and the enlarged eyes pop out. But the other made no attempt to withdraw. 'Get away, will you!' he said angrily.

The man moved his pointed tongue over his lower lip. 'Can I do anything for you – anything at all?'

'Take out your head till I shut the door.'

79

'All right, boy, all right! But if you ever want a – friend,' he closed one bulbous eye and smiled, 'Phil Turner's your man.'

He withdrew his head suddenly and allowed the door to close. But his soft shuffle could be heard outside as he sidled about. He was still there when Richard pulled the chain and came out. Phil smiled ingratiatingly, like someone claiming a prior acquaintance, and watched him down the corridor.

Commander Barnwell's door was open and the Commander himself was sitting up in bed, leafing through a magazine with a large sailing ship on the cover.

'Good morning,' Richard said. 'I'm coming to see you for a change.'

'Splendid!' The Commander smiled and laid aside his magazine. 'Take a pew.' He reached out to remove some papers from the chair and Richard sat down.

'On your feet again, eh? How does it feel?'

'A bit groggy, I'm afraid,' Richard said ruefully.

'Never mind. You'll find your sea legs in no time.'

'How are you today?'

'Like a mainsail in a sou'wester,' the Commander fretted. 'Full of wind.'

'Still as uncomfortable as ever?'

The Commander laid his hand on his inflated stomach. 'Blown up like a bloody bladder,' he said.

There was a shuffling on the corridor outside and the face of Phil Turner, like an errant moon, peered in.

'Be off!' the Commander shouted. 'I told you I didn't want any of your damned nostrums.'

The face shot out like a kicked football and disappeared.

'Who's that fellow?' Richard asked.

'Damned if I know,' the Commander said crossly. 'Tried to sell me some patent medicine. Guaranteed cure, he said, at thirty bob the bottle.' He reached down in to the bed and pulled up a flat quart of whiskey. 'Now, if it had been this kind of bottle!'

He was about to uncork it when the brisk gait of Sister Cooney was heard on the corridor. He shoved it down between the sheets again and held his finger to his lips. 'I hear the admiral on the quarterdeck,' he said. 'Watch out, or we'll be keelhauled!'

Richard rose unsteadily. 'I'd better be off.'

'I was about to offer you a drop – to celebrate,' the Commander whispered. 'Later, perhaps, eh?'

'Sure!' Richard smiled. 'I'll be back.'

It was very hot in the back of the ambulance and Lily was inclined to be sick. Marty, the ambulance man, had a way of dashing up to corners and standing on the brakes before going into them that flung them about a lot. With Marty, every journey was an emergency run and he arrogantly blasted other traffic aside with blaring klaxon.

They were subdued on the way down, except for Ted Nugent, brash and self-confident as usual, a man who had come singing mellifluously from the womb, blessed and chrismed with charismatic speech. Ted expertly drew them together in an amiable lasso of blather. There were six of them altogether – Lily, Mrs Doran, and four men. Of the four, Lily was acutely aware of one. Vincent sat opposite her at the other end of the seat, nearest the door. Their eyes met occasionally and they smiled, the polite, shy smile of people lumped together by circumstance rather than choice.

They had met once or twice outside the treatment room while waiting for a refill, and had exchanged glances or a few pleasantries. But mainly their reality for each other had been in words.

They had never seen each other out of dressing gowns before – were not even sure of each other's identity when their eyes met across the width of the ambulance. She thought he looked smart in his navy suit and red tie. But his shirt collar was too loose and his face under the dark hair was pale.

She tried to piece his letters to his expression. There had been a flow of them over the weeks – letters written in all kinds of moods. She liked him in his cheerful, flippant mood, where he thumbed his nose at misfortune, or told of Arty's latest entanglement. But there was a deeper, more serious, Vincent who appealed to her much more. She recognised in him some of her own probing, puzzled response to life. They were like two people adrift together on a raft – no more likely to make a landfall than if alone, but cheered and comforted by each other's presence.

Vincent felt shy in her company. He blushed at the thought of how confidently he had written. When she had told him about Joe and his betrayal (with a deal of heart-searching before and misgivings after), Vincent had boasted that one day they would walk up Joe's street together and promenade in front of his door, until the message got through his thick skull that she had no further need of him.

Nurse Bodkin, a middle-aged widow with glasses and a perpetually surprised look, sat in front beside Marty and glanced back occasionally to see if they were all right – her round, startled face filling the glass. Ted, who had found it easy to persuade her that she was a fatally attractive woman and a threat to the virtue of even the most moral male, waved his hand airily at her, and she smiled a fat smile that crept and lingered over her face like a complacent slug. It was important to keep Nurse Bodkin happy if they were to make a stop at the wayside pub.

Lily sat demurely with her hands in her lap, her eyes on the ribbed rubber flooring, only raising them now and again to steal a glance at Vincent. She had told him all about the shop and her ambition to have a little business of her own – a fashion shop or, perhaps, a children's shop, which the town badly needed. He had encouraged her, because he too had no intention of spending his life working for someone else. There were plenty of opportunities for people with courage and initiative.

Both knew that their plans were flawed by the insidious disease, burrowing like a mole inside them. Of this they did not – and could not – write. But they were conscious of it all the time. It shadowed their every mood and threatened the future. Death was all around them, culling victims as unpredictably as the fall of dice. At best, a groundless optimism supported them, a hope that somehow when the house collapsed, they would be found standing unharmed amongst the rubble.

Vincent felt awkward in his suit, like a countryman on Sunday. He was so used to flopping about in slippers and dressing gown, had so got out of the way of wearing more formal attire that he felt encased in armour. He kept running his finger around the collar of his shirt, though as Lily had observed, it was looser than it should have been.

After the x-rays, Ted had taken Nurse Bodkin in hand and her girlish laughter rang along the corridors until he had teased and flattered her into munificence. Persuading Marty was no trouble. He liked stopping at pubs. He found it profitable. With the glowing butt of a cigarette burning his lip, he would leap out and line up at the counter and wait quietly to be asked to name his drink. He would surprise them all by saying that he was not allowed to drink on duty, but had no objection to taking twenty cigarettes. When the cigarettes were served, he would open the pack and light a fresh one from the stub of the old and sigh with satisfaction and ease himself into weighty conversation. Every time a round was called, Marty pocketed his twenty cigarettes, and when it came to his turn, he consulted his watch in a brisk, professional way and decided it was time to be making tracks.

Lily was glad of the stop. She felt sick and in need of air. As soon as Marty had opened the double doors and let down the steps, he had stood aside while the men descended and followed them into the pub. He was a stickler for protocol. Last in, first out was a winning and – if questions should be asked later – a face-saving formula.

Vincent stood by the doors uncertainly and watched the men go in. He was in no hurry to follow them. Inside the ambulance Nurse Bodkin had pushed back the window and was talking to Mrs Doran. Lily had moved down the seat and was leaning out, breathing deeply, her face very pale.

'Would you … like anything?' Vincent asked diffidently.

'I don't feel well,' Lily said.

'Maybe you'd like to get out?'

Lily nodded. He held out his hand to help her down the steps. She took it hesitantly and emerged into the sunlight. After the noise of the engine, the silence was acute. Vincent dropped her hand awkwardly and stood beside her, his fingers tingling from the contact.

'You'll feel better in a minute,' he said solicitously.

'I think … I'm going to be sick.'

'Could you walk a little?'

She nodded and he led her slowly down a lane that ran beside the gable of the pub. When she seemed to falter, he put protective hands about her shoulders and urged her on until they rounded a bend and were out of sight of the road. He supported her as she leaned over and retched drily into the long grass.

'If you could be sick, you'd feel better,' Vincent said.

For a while she hung suspended, dribbling into the ditch. The only sound was the beat of a grasshopper and a warm sigh in the leaves overhead.

'I'm all right now.' Lily straightened up. Her face was white with a green underlay. Limp strands of hair clung to her forehead. 'I feel a little weak,' she said.

Close by, under the sycamores, a stile crossed the ditch into a meadow. Vincent helped her forward and she sat on one of the broad flags.

'Thank you,' she whispered.

Out in the meadow with startling suddenness a voice creaked, cracking and breaking like the snap of sticks.

'Corncrake!' Vincent said with passionate intensity, somewhere in his deep subconscious the image of a free spirit ranging through the grass.

'Summer!' Lily responded. 'You could hear them in the fields behind our house on hot summer nights.'

'I know,' Vincent said. 'Time to go swimming again.'

'We used lie awake in the long evenings with the window open, listening,' Lily remembered.

'Always corncrakes in the fields by the river,' Vincent said.

The voice stopped as abruptly as it had started. They were aware of each other again in the silence.

'Feel better?' Vincent asked.

Lily smiled. A little colour had returned to her cheeks. 'Much better, thank you. It's nice here, isn't it?'

Vincent nodded several times without speaking. He kicked at the grass and examined with great curiosity a white blob of cuckoo spit that clung to his toecap. In the field the corncrake rasped harshly again.

'Wouldn't it be nice to sit here all afternoon and forget everything?'

'If only we could!' Vincent said vehemently.

'To walk around that corner,' Lily continued in a dreamy voice, 'and find no ambulance there ... '

'And all the rest just a nightmare,' Vincent said.

Silence again, as heavy with sighs as the shifting currents of air, heavy as the many-scented, somnolent afternoon.

'Lily,' Vincent said tentatively, 'if we ever get out of this, I'd like ... to see you again.'

'I'd like to see you too,' Lily said simply.

She made room for him on the stile and he sat down beside her. He took her hand awkwardly and held it in his, and for both of them the whole quality of the day changed.

Out in the meadow the corncrake cranked himself up for a major statement. Then a mowing machine started up, ringing musically as it turned into the corners. The corncrake stopped, sensing danger. For a while he would crouch in an ever-lessening island of grass. Later, in desperation, he would run before those triangular, slicing blades. He might – or might not – escape.

They sat and listened as the sound filled the great copper dome of the sky, drowning the delicate stir of leaf and hedgerow. When it rounded the field and bore heavily down on them, Lily stood up and sighed. 'We'd better be getting back.'

They walked slowly down the lane, holding hands until they reached the turn, both aware of the metal beat of the mowing machine behind them, cutting down their afternoon.

8

'One thing is certain,' Doctor Staples said. 'You can't cure a fool of TB.'

The young nurses, gathered in his office to listen to him, giggled a little nervously, then overcompensated by straightening up and looking solemn. It was his custom to lecture them occasionally on various aspects of the disease. He stood before them in his familiar pose with his left hand in the pocket of his white coat – thumb protruding.

'What do I mean by fool? I mean anyone who does not follow scrupulously – I might even say religiously – the regime laid down for him here. It is, therefore, the prime duty of every nurse to insist on adherence to this regime. Without it, none of our patients can survive.'

He paused to give them time to digest his words.

'I'd like to quote you the dictum of a famous medical man, who had in his care the health of thousands – hundreds of thousands – of people, Surgeon-General Bushnell of the US Army. This is what he said – and I give you his exact words: "For TB we prescribe not medicine but a way of life."'

'Now, the whole purpose of the treatment here is to teach patients that way of life – that disciplined daily routine. It's a monotonous routine, but a necessary one. What I'm saying is that this is as much a school as a hospital, and what a patient learns here he must go out and practise for the rest of his life. The trouble with TB is that it's rarely detected early enough to be cured completely. But it can be arrested and held in check, and this is where the discipline comes in. A patient can look forward to a long life – a restricted life, of course, but, at least, a life – if he learns this regime and sticks to it. It's not easy. No one ever said it was. It's like going on a diet – a permanent diet. Easy enough for a while, but to stick to it, day after day, year after year, requires real courage and endurance. Plus, of course, intelligence – intelligence to realise that it's his only hope. And that brings me back to where I started. You can't cure a fool of TB.'

When they had gone and he was left alone with Sister Cooney, he shook his head gloomily. He always felt gloomy after his talk on the regime. The whole thing was unrealistic. It was one thing to follow it under supervision in a hospital, quite another to do the same thing outside. Besides, how many of his patients could afford to coddle themselves like that when they went out? They were fathers of families with mouths to feed, harassed mothers of young children, young men and women who had to make their own way in life.

The regime was all right for leisured folk – Barnwell and his type – who could afford to build a chalet in some sheltered place in the garden and keep regular hours and have good meals and fresh air and sunshine and no worries – the kind of self-indulgent, pampered folk who had no qualms in leaning on others and whose hermitage could be supported by servants and friends.

'The sooner someone makes that dictum of Bushnell's obsolete, the better,' he said. 'What we want for these people is medicine – and to hell with his way of life!'

88

'Aren't they experimenting with some new drugs?' Sister Cooney asked.

'Yes, they're experimenting all the time. I've been reading a very promising report in the BMJ on a drug called streptomycin.'

'I suppose it will be years, though, before we see it here?'

'No, actually. The new Minister, Noel Browne – there's a man for you! – is on the ball. They're trying it out in Peamount already. We may be able to lay our hands on some sooner than you think. I'd like to see what it can do for a few of our younger patients.'

The thought of being a pioneer in the field, of pushing back the frontiers of ignorance and superstition that surrounded the disease, of bringing hope where there was none, cheered him a little. He was so used to seeing himself as custodian of a mortuary that any prospect of a cure was encouraging.

'Do you think there's anything in it?' Sister Cooney asked.

'There may be,' he said cautiously. Then his face darkened again and he shook his head slowly back and forth, tightening his lips as he did it. 'Trouble is, it will come too late for most of the present lot.'

It was a lonely time after the letter had been written. Richard stood at the window sometimes, watching the high, troubled clouds, like souls cut adrift, moving forever out of his vision, out of his life. There was no stability anywhere. All was flux, change, decay.

Away below him in the valley, the river slid on its mystical, restless quest. Only down in its depths, where the wise, polished stones clung to their reality, was there no memory of change. But even there, if one were to refine curiously on the matter, there was displacement, erosion, anomaly.

Though he was hardly conscious of it, he had wanted her to

89

insist, to storm in and overwhelm his considerate prudence with a cry from the heart that went beyond wisdom and caution to the root of a shared experience. But because she was too young, too unsure of herself and him, she had failed to read the plea beneath the surface of his letter, and had kept a sad, puzzled silence. There was no reply, and as the weeks passed, he had come reluctantly to accept that there would be none.

To keep himself from brooding and lapsing into despair, he began to read. The library, such as it was, was a strange hotch-potch of books. Some had come with the house; some had been donated by well-meaning charitable organisations; a great number were unclaimed books from the lockers of dead patients.

For the best part of a month, he plodded through a copy of *Mein Kampf*, immersing himself in *Weltanschauung* and *Lebensraum*, fascinated by the warped fanaticism that had made and unmade the world in which he had grown up. There was something about the clotted, convoluted reasoning that repelled and terrified him. It was like lying with a madman astride his chest, shrieking and foaming at the mouth, beating his head against a rock, until he had battered him into an acceptance of his manic vision.

Yet, he had returned to it again and again. He had never really thought about the human race or its potential before. He had never really thought very deeply about anything. He had been in school during those years and Hitler had been no more than a comic bogeyman, goose-stepping across a map of Europe. Now he began to see him as the Antichrist of the twentieth century, and this book, his foul, prophetic testament.

Hitler had been only one of the many forces of evil in the world – the most reviled because the most spectacular. Death stalked the corridors outside as it had at Belsen or Dachau. The difference was simply one of number and cause. There, hundreds of thousands; here, a slow, pernicious trickle. Here, blind chance, cruel fate, or what complacent fools, with no intimation of mortality in their guts, were pleased to call the hand of God; there (*homo* – as ever – *homini lupus*), the murderous hand of man.

Faced squarely, though, the unpleasant fact was that there was no difference in cause. The hand in both cases was the hand of man. His disease was a social one. It thrived on bad housing, appalling working conditions, exploitation, poverty, ignorance. Money that might have gone towards medical research went instead for armaments. As long as bishops lived in palaces and tinkers in tents, as long as some rode high in limousines and others crawled like insects in the gutter, as long as men could view with complacency the degradation of their fellow men, it was the worst kind of hypocrisy to ascribe evil in the world to an indifferent or malicious diety. The fatal flaw in human society was the ice at the heart of man himself.

Dear Mr Finn,

There must be some mistake. I have read newspaper accounts of the motor racing at the Phoenix Park and there is no mention in any of them of an accident, or of anyone being killed. I've been getting a number of odd letters about Arty lately. Someone seems to be having a good laugh at my expense. If Arty is tired of writing and is using this way to get rid of me, he should have the courage to write and tell me decently. But I don't think he'd do a thing like that to me. He's too nice a fellow –

'Whee-ee!' Arty shouted. 'Some woman, that Madeleine!'
'Some stupid cow!' Vincent said. 'Let me finish it, will you? "… too nice a fellow to fool about –" ' Vincent raised his head, 'God but she's innocent!' then read on:

I believe somebody wants to end things between us and is

91

deliberately hiding my letters from him and writing this terrible and malicious rubbish to me. They said he was rich and that I was after his money. This is a terrible lie. I would love Arty if he were the poorest of the poor and the lowest of the low.

Vincent teased, 'But he is girl! He is!'

'Christalmighty!' Arty exclaimed. 'The woman is stark, raving mad!'

'Wait!' Vincent held up his hand. 'There's more.'

Please, Mr Finn, help me to find the truth. I believe you are his friend, because he has often mentioned you in happier days. Please arrange for me to meet him. If I hear from his own lips that he doesn't want to know me any more, I'll go away and never trouble him again.

'Well, Arty boy, what are you going to do about that?'

'I'm dead – and I'm staying dead,' Arty said.

'How can you stay dead if she won't believe it?'

'I'll die all over again – only this time it'll be more convincing. Get out your pen and write another letter.'

'You can write it yourself. I've had enough.'

'You're forgetting. I'm supposed to be dead. Just one more, Vincent, please.'

'Oh, all right! But if you have to be killed a third time, you can do it yourself.'

'There won't be any third time if you do it right. No more of your cod-acting about being buried at sea. Dying is a serious business and you ought to know it.'

'Tell me what to say, then.'

'Tell her you got the facts wrong the first time from the distressed relatives. Say of course I wasn't killed in the race. That was a stupid thing to say. Say I was killed on the way home after the race – fatigue or whatever. Say I drove off the road over a cliff into a bottomless quarry. Say the body was never recovered. That ought to settle her.'

9

The sun sang in the magic of its rising for Lily Moore. It came over the hill with the rush of a lover, pushed warmly in beside her on the pillow where she lay, and flared out in fire from her combed hair. All day and every day it shone, prodigal, prodigious, wheeling in a great arc round her, lingering by night, like a retained image on the retina, to illuminate her dreams.

She was up early now, dancing to an old tune. Her voice was as light as her footsteps on the corridor. Through the bright days she floated and drifted and swooned like thistledown on summery currents, up, up and away.

When she wasn't talking to Vincent from the verandah or from the bathroom window – running foul of Sister Duggan's tongue – she was writing to him. She sat for hours, propped in bed, a rapt flush of concentration on her face. She smiled as she wrote, stopping often to reread and amend. Sometimes she laid the letter aside and sat hugging her knees, while she made a dreamy survey of the landscape, seeing only that leafy lane and listening for the free, life-asserting call of the corncrake.

Elsie, too, had heard that call. She was well enough now to go downstairs to the dining room for her meals. But she had been able to get no further. The next step was to be allowed to walk in the grounds for an hour, from eleven to twelve. When she asked permission, she was refused. Walking in the grounds and discharge would come in their own good time. Meanwhile, she must be patient. Patience was a small price to pay for a lasting recovery. Elsie listened to the voice of reason – so detached, so unemotional. What did Doctor Staples, who had never lost his freedom, know of the wild call of summer and of hot young men.

She began to mope and turned out from the ward to the insistent pulse of the countryside. She leaned over the verandah, her hand under her chin, drugged by the promise of that beckoning sky. Her body was heavy with unfulfilled desires, weighed down with unappeased longings and heady languors that stung and teased.

One busy afternoon, when the wards were full of visitors, she quietly packed her things, put on her best clothes, and slipped out without saying goodbye to anyone. Down the avenue she went, never looking back, like a sleepwalker absorbed in dreams. The quickening air, benign on her body, drew her on, her spirit joying in its natural element.

Her absence was discovered at tea-time. Such defections were not unusual. She was over twenty-one and nothing could be done. Her bed was stripped and remade in preparation for the next patient. Nobody was surprised when the rumour went about that it was for someone whose brother was upstairs. Once entrenched, the disease worked its way like woodworm through a household.

'Did you ever find yourself wondering,' Frank asked, as he stood at the railings, looking out over the darkening land, 'whether it's a mirage out there, whether there's anything left in the world only this crazy hulk, foundering here in the fields?'

'I know what you mean,' Vincent sighed. 'Maybe you'll find out tomorrow.'

'You wonder if you ever had another life, if it all wasn't just a dream.'

'Drink up, old son,' Vincent said. 'Maybe this is the mirage – or maybe we're in hell and don't know it.'

'That's a cheerful thought!' Frank smiled. He turned to look back into the ward. A number of men and boys had gathered there, sitting on the beds in the twilight, talking quietly. There was a fug of smoke about and the warm smell of porter. Bottles stood on the lockers and empties lay on the floor. The scene moved him. They had saved up their daily bottle of stout to give him a little sendoff. Celebration or wake? he wondered morosely.

Down through the darkening ward, he could see Sister Cooney in the lighted office. She was good about things like this. There was humanity in her. She was on the side of life. The men had been allowed to save their bottles for a few days, though it was strictly against the rules.

'Well, how does it feel, Frank?' someone asked.

'Tomorrow to fresh woods and pastures new,' Frank said. 'I'll tell you how it feels. I'm beginning to understand that saying about the frying pan and the fire.'

'There's hope – or something – where you're going, anyway,' Phil said.

'Or something!' Frank said without enthusiasm.

'Don't worry, Frank, boy,' Arty said. 'We'll see you back here in eight or ten weeks, a new man – and after that it's a short step to the door.'

Arty was sitting up in bed, his scalp shining, his short hair stiff as a nailbrush. He had his accordion around his neck and was running his fingers over the keys.

'Give us a tune, Arty, and forget the sentiment,' Frank said. 'It's bad for the dandruff.'

Arty launched suddenly into a lively tune and the men tapped out the rhythm with their feet. Frank saw Sister Cooney glance towards them, then smile to herself as she turned back to her work. She would intervene only to protect the very ill or to forestall objections from below.

'Fine, Arty. Fine!' Frank said. 'Only – turn down the volume a bit, would you?'

Arty nodded and drifted into something quiet and melancholy.

'Many's the good man never came back,' Jack Carbery whispered to Phil.

'Jem Poole, sure,' Phil said.

'Aye, Jem! I remember well the night before Jem, God be good to him, went. We were sitting around just like this.'

'And Stevie,' Phil said. 'You knew Stevie?'

'I knew them all.' Jack was aggrieved that anyone should presume to know more about the place and its patients than he did. 'I knew everyone that came or went this twenty year!'

'Sure you did,' Phil said, apologetic as usual. 'Nobody better!'

'That's a nice little girl you've got below,' Frank said to Vincent, where they still stood on the verandah, their faces no longer clearly defined. 'A very nice girl. Stick to her, boy.'

'She's a grand girl,' Vincent agreed, his face clouding. It was several days since he had seen her. She had complained of chest pains and breathlessness and been put on strict bed rest. Doctor O'Connor-Crowley had diagnosed fluid, and had berated her soundly for being caught out of bed. She had been moved to a single room on the corridor to keep her away from the temptation of the verandah. He felt guilty and anxious, blaming himself for her indiscretion.

'It's a woman makes or breaks a man,' Frank was saying. He was in a confiding mood. The fact that he was on his way elsewhere and might never see Vincent again made it easier to speak. The friendly darkness pressing in across the fields was also a help. 'I don't mind telling you I made a mess of things myself,' he said.

Vincent clucked sympathetically, not knowing what else to do.

'My own fault, though! I must say that. It always is your own fault, you know.'

'How come?' Vincent asked.

'You either make an error of judgement at the very beginning – make the wrong choice – or you let something good die, because you're too stupid or too selfish to work at it and keep it alive. Either way, it's your own fault.'

'I suppose so,' Vincent said. He felt there was some positive response he should make, but didn't know what it was. It would be presumptuous to tell the man that he felt sorry for him. Pity was a weak prop to offer anyone. Frank wasn't speaking as if he pitied himself, and would hardly be grateful for pity from others. He was just stating facts, giving Vincent the benefit of his experience. But Vincent felt sorry for him, all the same. Frank had been a sane friend and deserved better. No man should be left to face life – not to speak of death – alone. 'Isn't is possible to … patch things up again?' he ventured.

'I suppose so,' Frank agreed. 'Just as you can patch up a leaky boat and – with a bit of luck – finish the voyage. But you're so busy bailing water and worrying about whether you'll make it that there's no time left to enjoy the journey.'

'But isn't it better than nothing?' Vincent asked.

'Maybe,' Frank agreed sourly, 'provided your partner doesn't decide to abandon ship.'

The bottles were all empty now and the men began filtering back to their wards. Arty brought the music to a stop with a flourish, unstrapped the accordion and laid it aside. Sister Cooney, a light cardigan thrown over her shoulders, came briefly in to say goodnight and wish Frank well, before going off duty. The slow, incantatory murmur of men saying the rosary came from one of the wards.

'Time for bed,' Vincent said. He stretched himself slowly and yawned. Unloosening the belt of his dressing gown, he strolled in. 'Come on, Frank,' he said. 'You'll get cold out there. Tomorrow is another day.'

'From the evils of tomorrow, good Lord, deliver us!' Frank said.

He turned out towards the black fields and the velvet, far-starred sky. A flit and drift of white from the massed bulk of trees caught his eye. Death was out there, fanning over the grass and fear was a mouse burrowing into the roots. The faint owl hoot, when it came, was full of menace. He shivered and drew his shoulders closer together. Overhead, the mind-shattering stars put life and death and time into perspective.

'I say, Mildred, old girl,' Commander Barnwell began briskly, as soon as the preliminaries were over and his wife had sat down, 'I've been doing some hard thinking – about Clover Lodge, I mean.'

His wife paused in slotting a cigarette into her black holder to look at him shrewdly. 'The wanderlust getting into you again, Percy?' she asked.

'Look at it this way, old girl,' the Commander said. 'You can't go on managing the place on your own. It's too big. I've been thinking we should sell out and buy a little place in Falmouth or Littlehampton. What do you say?'

'We'll talk about it when you get better, dear,' Mildred said in a placatory tone.

'Now is the time to talk.'

'There's plenty of time, dear. No hurry in the world.' She lit her cigarette and tilted her lugubrious jaw to blow smoke towards the ceiling.

'Get Maunsell to advertise the place,' he said. 'Put it in all the quality papers – British I mean, of course.'

'We mustn't do anything precipitate,' Mildred cautioned.

'Play up its attractions – the fishing rights on the Owenascawl –'

'That's just it, Percy, dear. You know how fond you are of the fishing.'

'The shooting – grouse, snipe, partridge, pheasant – that kind of thing. Residence of character. Georgian residence of character. There's something attractive about the word 'Georgian'. Justifies putting a few hundred extra on the asking price.'

'And the ground damp?' Mildred asked, raising her eyebrows.

'No need to mention that, m'dear. They'll find that out soon enough. Ground damp will be no problem to a man of means. Just the kind of little challenge to occupy him between the fishing and the shooting.'

'Really, Percy!' Mildred smiled. 'Have you no morals?'

'Morals, old girl,' Percy wheezed, 'are a luxury we poor folk can't afford.'

Mildred looked at his sunken cheeks, the skull a harsh reality beneath the skin. Her faded eyes flickered with concern. He didn't seem to be making any progress, or to be aware of his true condition.

'How have you been keeping, dear?' she asked in an attempt to change the subject.

'Land in good heart. Don't forget that,' Percy said. 'The ads always talk of land in good heart.'

'I know.' Mildred smiled. 'Puts a couple of hundred extra on the asking price.'

'Get on to him this evening. Remember, now.'

'How have you been keeping, dear?' she asked again.

'Damned uncomfortable,' he said, 'like one of those inflatable rubber dinghies. Can't eat – nauseated all the time.'

'Poor dear!' Mildred touched his arm gently. 'Maybe you should ask them to discontinue it.'

'Only did it to please you,' Percy said.

'I know, I know,' she sighed. 'Maybe I was wrong.'

'Stick it a little longer,' he said stoutly, 'to see if it does any good. If not, time to change tack.'

'Would you like me to have a word with the doctor about it?'

'Already speaking to him,' Percy said. 'Decent enough chap – sympathetic. Says it's a slow process. Keeping it under constant review. I'm afraid, old girl, I'm getting a bit old for all this internal knocking about.'

Mildred laid her cigarette holder on the ash tray and, turning aside, busied herself with her basket on the floor. She spent quite a while fumbling over it, before raising it to her knees and saying brightly, 'Look, dear, I brought you a little brandy.'

Percy reached for the bottle eagerly and laid it under the blanket beside him.

'I know it's not good for you,' Mildred dabbed her moist cheeks with a wispy handkerchief, 'but you must have something.'

Percy looked at her, a little surprised at first by her display of feeling, and then patted her hand lightly. 'Cheer up, old girl,' he said. 'That's the spirit.' Then seeing the latent pun in his remark, he affected a gaiety he did not feel and held up the bottle. 'Brandy

– that's the spirit!' He chuckled thickly and began to cough. When the spasm had subsided, he pointed to a clean glass on the locker. 'Here, pass me that medicine glass.' He poured a little in and handed it to her. 'Do you good,' he said. 'Take it.'

Mildred took the glass and sipped it slowly. He watched her with growing impatience until she had finished, then reached for the glass and poured a stiffer dose for himself. He sniffed at it, held it up to the light and smiled.

'Down the hatch!' he said and swallowed it.

Afterwards he made her wash the glass with water from a jug on the locker and throw the contents out the window. 'We don't want them nosing about,' he said. Then settling himself back more comfortably on the pillows, he returned to his original theme.

'Now, about Maunsell ...' he began.

10

He had dreamed of it once and woke, oppressed with the weight of guilt. They had all been lying there, wasted under the pale sheets, their sunken eyes shadowed like pits. He had walked between the beds and craved their forgiveness, but they had turned away – their heads lolling on their necks like wilted flowers. His father's fingers, grotesquely clubbed, scrabbled at the coverlet. Then with a gurgle and a rush of red, like death bursting into bloom, they had collapsed one by one – his mother and father and Eileen and Michael and Liam – and their flesh had fallen away and Sister Cooney had come to pull the sheets over their bones, and he had slunk off, the murderer of his own kind, the sower of the fatal seed that had destroyed them all.

Michael came alone to tell him. It had always been Michael's lot, as the eldest, to be the bearer of bad news. Whenever misfortune or disaster struck, he had been sent to inform relatives and neighbours. It was an imposition that he dreaded. Over all the years he had never developed a suitable formula for his revelations.

'It's Eileen,' he said, locking and unlocking his hands. They stared at each other in silence, until it became unbearable and Michael rose to stand by the window. 'She'll have to come in here.' He opened the window out fully and stared over the red tiles down into the gutter, as if he were searching earnestly for something. Then he half-closed the window carefully and turned back into the room. 'We all got a clean bill of health only Eileen. Something on her x-ray.'

'How bad?' Richard asked with heavy foreboding.

'Bad enough. I don't know,' Michael shot back impatiently to hide his distress.

'What did the doctor say?'

'You know doctors! Tell you nothing. She had some kind of test – her spit … '

'Sputum test?'

'I suppose so. It was bad anyway.'

'Positive?'

'Of course I'm positive!' Michael deflected his grief into anger.

'I mean the test. You say it was positive?'

'It was bad. That's all I know.'

Michael spoke gruffly, almost belligerently, as if he felt guilty too – as if being the bearer of bad news made him, somehow, the cause of it as well. It was like the time he had pulled Richard and Eileen from the river long ago and brought them home, shivering and dripping, and had been abused for not looking after them properly. Everyone seemed to forget that, but for him, they were lost, and for years he had gone about carrying with him the guilt of their almost-drowning. Life was hard on the eldest. When they did well, they were doing no more than their duty. When they failed, they were damned.

'When is she coming in?' Richard asked.

'She's below now. I came with her.' Michael turned away to the window again and stood tapping his nail on the glass. 'Christ!' he burst out suddenly. 'What kind of a rotten disease is it?' He turned with face averted and made for the door.

'Michael!'

He stopped without turning around.

'My mother and father – what way are they?'

'What way do you think they are!' Michael almost shouted. 'First you, and now Eileen!' He rushed out with his head down. Richard heard him stop on the landing and blow his nose stiffly. Then he came back slowly and stood at the door. 'I'll be in again,' he said. 'Do you want anything?'

'No. Tell them she'll be all right.'

Michael nodded without speaking.

When he had gone, Richard turned his head to the wall. It seemed to him that the whole world was breaking up. The thought of what lay ahead for Eileen, the loneliness, the despair, appalled him. Where could she find the resources that would be necessary to sustain her? How would she cope with that feeling of being built into a room, brick by brick? From where would she summon the act of will to push the walls out and keep them there? By what agonising process of trial and error might she learn the trick of retiring into the mind in order to relieve the pressure on the cramped body?

When Sister Cooney came round in the evening, he asked if he could be taken down to see her. She went off to enquire and returned after a long absence to tell him that the doctor was not available, but she would do her best to arrange for him to be taken down for a few minutes after breakfast the following morning.

When morning came, they insisted on bringing him down in a wheelchair, though he could walk well enough. Breakfast smells were everywhere and dust danced in shafts of sunlight where wardsmaids were sweeping on the corridor as they passed. He refused to be taken any further in the wheelchair than the door of the ward. It was important to walk in unassisted. To

see him so much recovered would give hope and encouragement to Eileen.

She was lying flat, her dark hair spread on the pillow. He was
shocked by the angularity of her features. All the roundness had
been leached out. When she smiled, her teeth seemed larger than
he had known them.

He sat beside her and took her hand and they looked at each
other in troubled silence.

'How are you?' he asked at length.

'How are you?' she asked by way of reply.

The act of speaking loosened some emotional restraint in her.
He watched helplessly as her composure crumpled and she
pulled up the sheet to dab her eyes. He pressed her hand and
tried to think of something encouraging to say.

'There are two of us now,' she sobbed. She turned her head on
the pillow and lay with her wet cheek against his hand.

'Don't, Eileen,' he said. 'Everything is going to be all right.'

'Will we ever get out of this place?'

'Of course we will. You and I are survivors. We survived the
river, didn't we? Remember the way Michael –'

'Michael could be the next,' Eileen cried.

Madeleine had written again. She was coming to find out the
truth. She was getting her holidays at the beginning of August
and would make the long journey by bus on the third, which was
a Wednesday. She would arrive in the late afternoon and hoped,
once and for all, to clear up 'this whole terrible mess'.

'What'll we do now?' Arty cried, every fibre atwitch.

'Do what you like,' Vincent said. 'I've had enough of this.'

'You can't let me down now. Just one last letter … '

'No more letters,' Vincent said firmly. 'The time for writing
letters is gone. Look at the date. Tomorrow is Wednesday.'

'Wednesday? What Wednesday?'

'The third of August. Tomorrow is D-day for you, boy!'

Arty clawed at his hair desperately, rubbing with his fingers until the scalp shone red. 'What am I to do?' he moaned.

'Tell her the truth. It's the simplest thing in the long run.'

'Simple!' Arty wailed. 'The simplest thing for me to do is die of the Con before she comes.'

From their beds the young women could see Mrs Doran taking exercise on the walks. Round and round she went, coming into their range of vision and moving out like the moon in orbit. There was something light and girlish about her step that pleased them and gave them hope. Occasionally she stopped to pluck something out of the hedge. She would come back, flushed and smiling, like a child after an adventure, bringing a little posy of wild flowers and tastefully selected leaves for someone's locker, a thoughtful gift that would shine there and sing of summer for an afternoon.

She would laugh and tell them how, behind the shelter of a screening hedge, she had slipped off her shoes and walked on the grass. Then she would reminisce about her girlhood, when she had skipped barefoot through the morning fields, turning in the sluggish cows, drugged with grass and rich summer scents. She remembered too – and kept the memory to herself – how, with the secret of her first-conceived stirring in the womb, she had gone out in her nightdress and felt at one with the teeming, maternal earth.

Doctor Staples had been pleased with her x-ray, and in a month or two, if her progress continued, she would return to the farm and the slow rhythms of the countryside.

Lily's progress had been less encouraging. The diagnosis of fluid in the pleural cavity had led to her confinement to bed and the painting of her chest with iodine. When such conservative methods of treatment had failed, Doctor Staples had made an exploratory puncture with a large hypodermic syringe and drawn off a sample of the fluid, which he sent to Dublin for pathological analysis.

When the report came back, she was taken down to the treatment room for aspiration. It was a painful experience – one she had since undergone several times. She was placed on the couch with a pillow under her right side and her arms drawn above her head which hung lower than the rest of her body. Her back was painted with spirit and ether. She was given a local anaesthetic, and when the area became numb, Doctor Staples, who had scrubbed up and donned rubber gloves, passed a slender cannula and trocar into the intercostal space, withdrew the trocar and drained off a pus-like fluid into a vacuum bottle.

Afterwards she felt faint and went through a stage of mild shock. She was taken back to bed on a trolley, given a little brandy to drink and wrapped in extra blankets and hot-water bottles. The operation was repeated within a few days and when, after several weeks, the condition persisted, Doctor Staples came, in his head-scratching, worried way, and explained that it might be necessary to send her to a larger sanatorium where they were better fitted to deal with her case. Lily heard him out impassively, but when he had gone, tears flooded her eyes and she turned to the wall in mute despair.

11

Day after drab day, Doctor O'Connor-Crowley barrelled through the wards like an angry wasp, competing with foul weather in the perpetual unpopularity contest, which her peculiar genius qualified her – and some strange inner compulsion drove her – to win. She worked her way like sand into the well-oiled, smooth-functioning machinery of hospital life, alienating staff, intimidating patients, causing friction and malfunction wherever she went.

Phil was the latest to fall foul of her ire. She had been stumping briskly from bed to bed and came at length to Phil, who lay, a supine mass of quivering eagerness, clasping his sweaty palms and ready to apologise for the crime of being still alive.

'Well, Turner,' she said, reading his name from the chart, 'how are you?'

'Fine, Ma'am, thanks,' Phil said, licking his nervous lips.

'Don't call me Ma'am. Call me Doctor,' she snapped.

'Yes, Doctor – Ma'am,' Phil stuttered, and began to twist the sheet into a knot.

She was about the pass on when her sharp eye fixed on Phil's open locker.

'Nurse,' she roared, 'fetch me those bottles.'

Nurse Bodkin, who was accompanying her, laid her bundle of charts on the trolley and bent down to remove three bottles of Harry Dagg's Special Herbal Elixir – Cure Guaranteed.

'Turner, what's this?' the doctor shouted.

'It's a cure – like,' Phil explained in an ingratiating whine.

She picked up one of the bottles and examined the label, her lip curling in disgust as she read. Phil watched her, his eyes darting about like frightened animals. He had got five more bottles after the initial one. He had dipped deeply into his savings to make the investment. Kielthy, who was to have been his partner in the venture, had backed out when neither of them had shown any marked improvement after taking the stuff. Phil had sold one bottle to a very sick patient who had since died. He had doled out most of another in sample spoonfuls to prospective customers, but as the price and the address were clearly marked on the label, those who were tempted to give the elixir a try preferred to send to Belfast for it themselves.

'Have you been taking this muck?' Doctor O'Connor-Crowley glared at him.

'A ... little,' Phil confessed in guilt-ridden tones.

'Cure guaranteed!' she said sarcastically. 'If it's guaranteed, why all the bottles?'

'I was ... ah ... getting some ... for the lads, like,' Phil confessed.

'Going into competition with the medical profession!' she bawled.

'Honest to God, Ma'am – Doctor – no!' Phil assured her in his most obsequious manner.

'I notice,' she sneered, 'this Mr Dagg is very careful not to give his medical qualifications.'

'I wouldn't say he's a doctor – like,' Phil ventured timidly.

'I see! Just an ignorant layman who happens to know more

than the whole medical profession put together! Did you know, Turner, you could be put in jail for peddling this poison?'

'It's not poison – whatever it is,' Phil asserted mildly, feeling himself on surer ground.

'Nurse!' Doctor O'Connor-Crowley ordered peremptorily. 'Take it out and pour it down the sink.'

'God, Ma'am – Doctor,' Phil wailed at the prospect of his loss, 'that's pouring away pound notes. Them's a quid a bottle.'

'Chalk it up to experience,' she told him sharply. 'And if I ever again hear of you sending for this stuff or trying to peddle it to my patients – my patients, Turner – I'll have you thrown out and prosecuted as well.'

'Oh, God, no Ma'am,' Phil quavered wetly, 'you'd never do that!'

'Wouldn't I though!' she said. 'What kind of stupid man are you! Don't you realise that this is just a confidence trick? There's nothing of any medicinal value in those bottles.'

When night came and the shadows thickened and solidified until he felt entombed in dark fears, he lay on his back, and closing his eyes, willed himself into the past. Like a diver thrashing downwards, he held his breath and clawed about for the entrance to the submerged cave that was memory. Within, there would be sand, shelving upwards to a chamber suffused with hidden light and resonant with echoes.

He had met her at a party. It was a simple, informal kind of party, whose purpose – if it had any – escaped him. He had gone along with a friend to someone's flat. They had brought things to eat rather than drink and had fried sausages and made tea and sat around on the floor, listening to gramophone records of Crosby and Sinatra and a new musical called *Finian's Rainbow*, and Hoagy Carmichael singing 'Buttermilk Sky'. There were about a dozen of them altogether, students from various faculties, known individually to their hosts, if not always to each other.

They had found themselves sitting side by side and began trading sandwiches – his egg for her tomato – and conversation. Later they danced – a dreamy shuffle to the music of 'Slow Boat to China' – with her hand laid lightly on his shoulder. She was not beautiful in any formal sense, but there was something warm and attractive about her when she laughed.

He surfaced again and the darkness lay heavy on him. He had brought up with him a memory of her hair. It was very black hair, black as Nurse Lambert's. There were other things about Nurse Lambert that reminded him of her. But he didn't want to think about them.

Down again. Down, down, down, into that bright bell of light. Eileen had black hair too – black hair with a natural curl that took easily to the permanent wave that was popular. On her sixteenth birthday, his father, who believed in independence and had already set Michael up in sheep, started her off in poultry. She already knew something about the subject, having just finished two years in a school for domestic economy, where she had studied the theory and practise of animal husbandry, poultry-keeping, cooking, and home management.

They had fenced in part of the haggard with wire netting and built two wooden chicken coops – with room for two more when the time came to expand. Her father bought a small oil-heated incubator with a one-hundred egg capacity, gave her ten pounds to cover such immediate expenses as eggs for hatching, fuel and food – and left her to it. The agreement was that within six months she would begin to supply the house with eggs and poultry – the latter being an easy task, since they rarely ate fowl. The profit from the sale of surplus eggs and chickens she would

112

keep to expand the business and lay the foundation for that nest egg she would put away in anticipation of her marriage.

Her first task had been to buy eggs of a pure-bred strain from an accredited poultry station. Her mother knew little of such matters and had been content enough all her life to raise a mongrel scratch of hens, more noted for their tenacity and endurance than for any strict or consistent dedication to egg-laying. She was inclined to favour Rhode Island Reds because they looked well and made a brave showing in the farmyard. But Eileen, who favoured White Wyandottes and Leghorns, had gone her own way and her mother had not interfered. On the contrary, she had agreed to sell off her own motley crew in the interests of preserving a pure strain, as soon as Eileen's first hatching matured and began to lay.

There had been great jubilation over that first tiny pullet's egg and when, soon after, a plump chicken, nicely browned and basted, came to table, her father had held aloft his mug of fresh buttermilk and toasted her success and given his solemn oath that she would do them all credit and bring prosperity to the man who was fortunate enough to get her.

She had invested some of her early profits in a sewing machine and started to make her own clothes. Then she had bought the bicycle on which she had come to visit him.

Down! Further down! Back into the inviolate, sun-and-moon-lustred past. Back into a childhood of blowing grass and swallows twittering cosily under the eaves, back to the hiss and spit of timber on an open hearth, to his father's stockinged feet widely spread, and to the soft shadow of his mother, warm and ample, moving about the kitchen.

12

Arty lay low in the bed, like a boat taking water. Every opening door, every distant footstep set up waves of shock that threatened to sink him.

'Any sign of her?' he hissed.

Vincent, sitting propped up in bed, his eyes on the outer ward and the corridor beyond, shook his head. 'Take it easy, Arty,' he said. 'Everything will be all right.'

Arty groaned and fingered his skull. It had seemed a good idea at the time to borrow a bandage from Nurse Lambert and swathe it about his head until only his eyes, nose and mouth were visible. Now he was not so sure.

'Do you think I should take this thing off? It's very hot.'

'No,' Vincent said. 'You're concussed. You've lost your memory. You're confused. Remember?'

'I'm too confused to remember,' Arty cried.

Strange voices outside sent him quivering beneath the blankets. Visitors were beginning to trickle in. Arty surfaced for a moment to plead: 'Couldn't you tell her you were me?'

Vincent put his finger to his lips and pointed to the corridor, where he had caught sight of Nurse Lambert in conversation with someone. He had told Lambert enough to enlist her sympathy and she had promised to keep an eye out for Madeleine and warn them of her arrival. 'Coming!' he hissed.

'God,' Arty prayed fervently, 'get me out of this and I'll never write a letter to a strange woman again.'

Vincent, who suddenly felt nervous himself, took out a cigarette and was busy lighting it when Nurse Lambert opened the door and announced very brightly, 'A visitor for you, Arty.'

She closed the door and went back to the office, leaving a big, amiable, red-haired girl standing uncertainly in the middle of the ward. Arty, who had his head resolutely beneath the blankets, held his breath.

Vincent drew on his cigarette warily and eyed her through a cloud of smoke. She looked over at him, and smiling broadly, came forward with her hand outstretched. 'You're Arty Byrne, aren't you?' she said. 'I'm Madeleine.'

Vincent shook his head violently and looked across towards Arty's bed. But apart from a submerged heaving, there was nothing visible.

Madeleine seized Vincent's hand and shook it. 'How are you?' she said. 'I bet you didn't think I'd come.'

She looked at him in a confident, challenging way and laughed. She wasn't at all the kind of silly nincompoop he had imagined she would be. For a second it flashed across his mind that she might be some friend of Lambert's whom she had sent to tease him.

'I …' Vincent began.

'You're a great hand with the letters,' Madeleine said and sat down on the bed.

Over her shoulder Vincent could see one wary eye surface above Arty's blankets. 'You've got the wrong man, you know,' he said.

115

'We laughed and laughed over them.' Madeleine laughed again at the memory.

'We? Who do you mean?' Vincent felt like a swimmer suddenly out of his depth.

'The girls at the switchboard. I did tell you I was a telephonist, didn't I?'

There seemed to Vincent to be a lot that she hadn't told them. 'I'm not Arty Byrne,' he said, 'if that's what you think.'

'Oh,'Madeleine said without embarrassment, 'you must be the other one, then.'

'I'm Vincent Finn.'

'The Venezuelan oil millionaire, I know!' she tapped him familiarly on the arm and giggled.

Over her shoulder Vincent saw Arty's bandaged head rising like a surprised moon. Whatever Arty had expected, it hadn't been anything like this friendly familiarity. He lay propped on his elbows, and strained to hear. But Madeleine's bent body screened their speech and only her laughter carried across the ward.

'You mean you had us taped all along?' Vincent felt relaxed enough to smile, since it was clear she had not resented the deception.

'We looked up Ardeevan in the telephone directory.'

'You were a step ahead of us all the way,' Vincent said ruefully, offering his cigarettes.

Madeleine took one and bent her red head towards the flame. She straightened up and blew smoke with an amused smile. 'It was great fun. We enjoyed it. I hope you did.'

'Oh, yes, yes,' Vincent assured her hurriedly, while deep in his mind another voice was saying: 'Some day I'll kill that Byrne!'

'Where is the great hero?' Madeleine enquired.

Vincent pointed to the bed where Arty was slowly subsiding

again under the moral weight of that accusing finger. Madeleine waved brightly at his drowning head and bounced up on her feet. 'I'd better introduce myself,' she laughed. 'Why is his head bandaged?'

'Another of his daft schemes,' Vincent said. 'The trouble that fellow dragged me into over you! You'd never believe it.'

'I'd believe it!' Madeleine said.

Vincent sat back and watched her approach Arty's bed. 'A visitor for you, Arty,' he called sweetly. 'Guess who?'

Madeleine stood at the foot of the bed and spoke to the heaving mass of blankets. 'Hello, Arty. I came, you see!'

A hand pushed the blankets aside and the worried, wary eyes of Arty looked up at her.

'I'm Madeleine,' she said and stretched out her hand. 'I'm glad to see you're ... alive ... after all!'

Amnesia, Arty's whirling brain urged, loss of memory, confusion, incoherence. God, why can't I drop dead? He drew himself up slowly and looked at her blankly. 'Are you from the Legion of Mary?' he asked in what he hoped was a remote, but courteous voice.

'I'm Madeleine and I've come a very long way to –'

'I have the leaflet,' Arty interrupted in a devout tone, 'and I say the prayers every day.'

'I've come to straighten things out with you – and your father,' Madeleine giggled.

Arty scratched desperately at his bandaged head. He would have to try something else. 'I'm sorry. I can't ... remember. I seem to have ... hurt my head.'

'Was that when you fell in the Grand National or the time you were killed in the Phoenix Park?' Madeleine laughed outright.

'I remember driving over a cliff ... ' Arty said slowly, as if the

117

memory was coming sluggishly and painfully. '"Twas the mercy of God –'

'You didn't drown?' Madeleine interrupted. 'I know! I was really worried about you that time. You'll have to give up this dangerous life.'

Arty felt himself more and more adrift. This wasn't the kind of girl he had imagined at all. This was a confident, attractive girl, who seemed to be making fun of him. What had Vincent and herself been laughing about? He looked over at him, but all he could see was Vincent's head ducking behind a newspaper.

'Pssst!' he beckoned to Madeleine as an idea came to him. 'That fellow you were talking to over there is all the time writing letters and putting other people's names to them. He's a bit – you know ...'

'What kind of hospital is this?' Madeleine asked, feigning alarm.

'It's a real loony bin, that's what it is,' Arty said.

'Are they all mental, then?' Madeleine asked delicately and looked over her shoulder at Vincent, who had dropped his paper and was watching them with a wide grin.

'Yeh, that's it!' Arty said, thinking he saw his way at last through the maze. 'Mad as coots the lot of them!'

'So,' Madeleine said in the tone of someone to whom all had been made plain, 'that explains all those wild letters?'

'Yes,' Arty agreed eagerly, 'that would explain them all, wouldn't it?'

'Only it doesn't!' Madeleine said sharply. Then, changing suddenly to a conversational tone, she enquired, 'How are the wife and children?'

'What?' Arty gasped.

'Surely you remember them?'

'I'm not married,' Arty protested.

'You must be a real far-gone case,' Madeleine giggled. 'Imagine, forgetting your poor wife and children!' She opened her bag and pretended to search in it. 'I have a letter here somewhere that might refresh your memory.'

'I hadn't hand, act or part in it,' Arty began excitedly. He sat up in bed and pointed to Vincent. 'Ask him. He knows all about it. He's the one to blame.'

'He only did what you told him,' Madeleine said.

Arty looked at her in desperation. She was a fine-looking girl in her own way, and under different circumstances, he might have been proud to have her talking to him. But now the whole thing was a mess. There was nothing for it but to tell her the truth and hope she wouldn't belt him to death with her handbag before storming out.

'Look,' he pleaded, 'don't get mad or anything, will you, if I tell you the truth.'

'Oh,' she said, 'your memory is coming back to you. Isn't that grand!'

'It was all a joke,' Arty explained, his hands pleading for understanding. 'We just did it for a cod.'

'Isn't it time you took off the bandage?' Madeleine said. 'You're beginning to sweat.' She stopped suddenly, as if a thought had struck her. 'You're not baldy under it – or anything?'

'No! No!' Arty protested, shocked into confusion at the suggestion. He started to pluck at the knot that kept the bandage in position.

'So, there was no Grand National?' Madeleine asked.

'No.' Arty was shamefaced.

'And no climbing Mount Everest?'

'I never said that!' he protested.

'Well, whatever mountain it was.'

'No.'

'And no work as a test pilot?'

'No.'

'And no discoveries in the Peruvian jungle?'

'No, nothing!' he said, wondering why she was taking it all with such equanimity. He had been unwinding the bandage as he spoke and sat with it, now, in coils before him.

'So, there you are!' she laughed. 'The great Arty Byrne – unmasked at last!'

She sat and heaved in generous, good-humoured bursts, while Arty stared at her in surprise and embarrassment.

'Did you hear that?' She turned to Vincent. 'He says it was all a joke.'

'We didn't see any harm in it, did we Vincent?' Arty pleaded for support.

'I know!' Madeleine wiped her eyes. 'It was all a cod!'

'It really was a joke,' Arty said earnestly. 'Tell her, Vincent.'

'What she's telling you is that the joke is on us,' Vincent explained. 'She knew all the time. She was just stringing us along – herself and her friends.'

Arty looked at her in disbelief. The contrast between the real Madeleine and the foolish, gullible Madeleine of the letters was so striking that he blushed at his preconceptions. He had been expecting some kind of daft, clinging ninny, some bizarre, free-floating escapist from a lunatic asylum. It was no easy matter to adjust his thinking to this cool, capable person who, it seemed, had had his measure and been laughing at him from the start.

'You knew all about this place and … everything?' he asked.

'Yes.'

'And you kept writing! Why?'

120

'We get bored too,' she said. 'Tell us,' she continued with a smile, 'were you worried about me coming?'

'No! No!' Arty said airily.

'Listen to him!' Vincent said.

'Well, maybe a little bit worried – in case you hadn't a sense of humour,' Arty conceded, and wondered why Madeleine and Vincent laughed so inordinately.

13

Lily liked the room with its apple-green walls and white ceiling which she was soon to leave. The move from the open ward and the verandah had not greatly troubled her. She wrote to Vincent every day and Mrs Doran and her friends still came to visit her.

She liked the privacy of the room. She liked to sit and dream and let those leafy walls bend and sway while her mind ran through summery tunnels into an eye of sunshine. The room was a glade, a breeze-blown bower, and she a lady stolen abroad to meet her lover. Her ardour whispered through her letters and sighed with the heat of fragrant afternoons. But sometimes, when she had written and waited impatiently for an answer, the room became a prison, a green jungle through which she beat with ineffectual hands and failed to find an exit. Yet mostly it was a pleasant place, a quiet centre around which she had begun to reorganise her life.

The news that she was to leave and go to another hospital was like an eviction order. She had had another x-ray and her case had been reassessed.

'As long as there's a trace of fluid, there's a danger of empyema,' Doctor Staples had told her. 'They're better fitted to deal with that at Seapark than we are.'

He had arranged to meet her mother and discuss the matter.

'How do you feel about it yourself, dear?' her mother asked her anxiously. 'Your father and myself are worried about you being so far away.'

'I'm confused,' Lily cried, her mind full of the pain of separation.

'You don't have to go, if you don't want to,' her mother soothed.

'But the doctor thinks it best,' Lily said.

'Yes, child. That's what he said. I'm afraid I didn't understand very much of what he said – you know the way doctors talk – but I did understand that much. He seems a good, careful man – concerned, like – the kind of man you could trust.'

When she told Vincent, he was troubled, but tried to reassure her. He had had a letter from Frank O'Shea, who had come successfully through the first stage of his thoracoplasty. Seapark was an optimistic, experimental place. They were using the new drug, streptomycin, there. Frank had been sprightly enough to joke about his condition. He had described himself as a little bent, a good deal bloody, but unbowed.

'I'll ask Father Paul in the friary to say a Mass, child,' her mother said.

'I'm lucky, really,' Lily smiled. 'There are people here a lot worse off than me.'

'I know, child!' Her mother blessed herself hurriedly. 'That poor young woman strapped to the frame for the best part of a year with TB of the hip and not able to move. God help her anyway.'

Eileen's hand was very dry to the touch and, like her nose and ears, was tinged with blue. Her breath came in shallow gasps. A pink blush burned on her cheeks, which were otherwise pale as

123

dried parchment – so dry that the skin looked as if it might burst into flame at any moment from the fire raging underneath.

'It's so hot,' she said weakly, her tongue moistening her chapped lips before she could speak.

'I know,' Richard said. 'I went through a fever like that too. Would you like a drink?'

He held the glass for her and supported her while she sipped. The change of position made her cough – a thick, burbling, mucus-laden cough. She turned aside to drool and dribble into the sputum mug.

'I'm sorry,' she gasped.

Richard squeezed her hand and watched with growing concern as she subsided on the pillows. 'You'll feel better after a while,' he said.

'How are you?' Eileen whispered.

'Don't mind about me. I'm all right.'

He had special permission to visit her for half an hour, two days a week. Sometimes he was asked to leave before the half-hour had passed, because she was very weak, and company – even his company – tired and excited her.

'Mammy says you were much worse at one stage.' Eileen turned towards him with her large, fevered eyes.

'Yes,' he said to encourage her. 'But I'm fine now. You'll feel better too, after a while. You'll see.'

He always left her with a feeling of despair, a dull pain that settled on him like a migraine and stayed until the next visit was due, when he was buoyed up again with the hope of finding her improved.

Once he had the courage to ask Doctor Staples about her.

'Your sister,' Doctor Staples had measured his words carefully, 'is a very sick girl. We are doing all we can for her.'

Richard had tried to put the rest of his fears into words, but could not. It was almost as if asking the question would some-how fix and finalise the disaster. As long as it remained unasked there was hope.

'You were pretty bad yourself, you know, when you came in,' Doctor Staples, who had read his faltering face accurately, had observed.

It was a little hope to cling to and Richard was grateful to him for offering it. Alone, he turned to prayer, assaulting heaven through the long days with a barrage of petition, sometimes raging ineffectually, shouting imprecations that boomed and reverberated inside the hollow of his skull, calling on a deaf God to listen, challenging His claim to be a wise dispenser of justice and mercy, beating helplessly at that huge, predetermined, cosmic will.

'Wouldn't it be nice,' Eileen said, 'to be sitting at home under the trees and never to have heard of this place at all!'

'Yes. If only we could turn the clock back. Do you remember how we used sit up in the big beech and listen to the wind in the leaves and pretend we were on a ship, sailing to some great adventure … ?'

'Yes,' she said, her eyes soft and remote.

'And Michael leaping from branch to branch, pretending he was a pirate about to board us …?'

'Yes,' she breathed gently, her eyes closed.

'And you were the captain, because Michael said if he couldn't be, I couldn't either …?'

A smile eased the tautness of Eileen's pinched face.

'And Liam on a little branch down below, because he was too small to be taken up any further …?'

'Happy days!' Eileen sighed.

'And my father shouting to know where we had all gone, because he needed someone to turn in the cows …?'

'Oh, Richard,' Eileen said, 'it's good to have been born and lived, if only for those times!'

'Remember the way we used get up early to pick mushrooms, creeping out without a sound?'

'Yes.'

'And the noise of the kitchen clock, ticking away in the silence, and the tracks of our feet through the wet grass, and the quiet, sleeping appearance of everything, and the sight of that first white mushroom –'

'The way we raced to get it!' Eileen said.

'And fought about who saw it first –'

'And trampled and broke it –'

'And then it didn't matter any more, because there were mushrooms everywhere.'

'The cherries,' Eileen said. 'Do you remember the cherries?'

'Wild cherries – along the ditch between the Far Field and the Long Moor –'

'God put them there, we said, especially for us –'

'And we poked them down with long sticks –'

'Or climbed after them until the branches broke.'

'The best ones were always at the top.'

' 'Twas this time of year, wasn't it?' Eileen said.

'Yes. The cherries should be ripe now.'

'Will we ever gather cherries together again, Richard?'

'Of course we will!'

He did not stop to wonder why his heart froze as he said it. The past – the safe and impregnable past – dropped away and blurred into a mist, while all before him, strewn with shards and flints, stretched deserts of desolation.

14

A bell in the office rang urgently and continued to ring. Sister Cooney, who was in the sluice room, heard it and came running. On a board underneath the bell a red light flashed beside the number of Commander Barnwell's room. Turning, she raced down the corridor.

The Commander was lying on his back. His mouth was open and his breath came in quick, shallow gasps. His left hand was clasped to his chest and he seemed to be in great pain. Sister Cooney reached for his wrist and felt his pulse. It was very light and rapid. She turned quickly to Nurse Lambert who had followed her down the corridor. 'I think he's had a collapse. Quick! Ring downstairs for O'Connor-Crowley. She should be somewhere on the female floor.'

Outside, the bell was still ringing. She eased the bulbous switch out of the Commander's right hand and it stopped.

'Don't try to talk,' she told him. 'We'll have you comfortable in a minute. I've sent for the doctor. She'll give you something to take away the pain.'

She loosened the neck of his pyjamas and checked his pulse more thoroughly. His breathing was very laboured, a series of strangled groans and pants.

'I think your lung may have collapsed,' she said. 'That's why you're finding it so hard to breathe. But don't worry – no, don't try to talk – the other lung will keep you going, as soon as it learns to adjust itself to the change.'

The Commander tried to articulate something and failed.

'It's better not to attempt to talk,' she told him. 'Just keep calm and concentrate on breathing.'

The lift clattered and shuddered outside, the gates screeched open and Doctor O'Connor-Crowley strode in. 'Well, Sister, what's the emergency?' she rasped in an aggrieved tone.

'Commander Barnwell has had a lung collapse – I think,' Sister Cooney said.

'You think!' Doctor O'Connor-Crowley said scornfully, still ruffled at the urgency of the summons.

'It's impossible to be certain, without proper examination, of course,' Sister Cooney replied stiffly. 'But it's probable, I should think. You must remember this patient has had a refill today.'

'I am well aware of that,' Doctor O'Connor-Crowley snapped. 'I gave it to him myself.' Then, as the full implication of Sister Cooney's observation struck her, she shouted angrily, 'Are you insinuating, Sister, that there was incompetence on my part? Are you saying that I gave this patient too much air and caused his lung to collapse?'

'I'm merely suggesting that if a lung is going to collapse, it's more likely to collapse after a refill than before,' Sister Cooney retorted sharply.

'You'll hear more of this!' Doctor O'Connor-Crowley ranted.

'My main concern at the moment is this patient,' Sister Cooney said. 'He is in considerable pain.'

'Why aren't you doing something, then?' the doctor cried. 'We'll need morphine.'

Sister Cooney stamped out stiffly, her legs rigid, the sound of her heels on the corridor like bullets exploding through glass. When she returned with the morphine and a syringe in a kidney dish, the doctor was putting away her stethoscope. 'We'll need a nurse to special this patient,' she said.

'Nurse Lambert will do it. She's on her way.'

When the morphine was administered, Commander Barnwell quickly passed into a drowsy state. The drug, depressing the sensory areas of the brain, reduced his pain. Although his breathing was still very laboured, it was a little more relaxed and the rate of his pulse began to slacken.

'Well, that's the best we can do for the moment,' Doctor O'Connor-Crowley said. She turned to Nurse Lambert who had arrived and was standing by. 'I want to be informed immediately about any change in the condition of this patient ... and Sister,' she continued sharply, 'I'd like some further words with you on this matter in the office.'

'That can wait,' Sister Cooney snapped. 'With one of my staff engaged here, I'm going to be very busy for the rest of the afternoon.'

'I insist!'

'If you have anything further to say, I'd prefer you said it in the presence of Doctor Staples when he comes tomorrow.' Sister Cooney busied herself about the Commander's bed, squaring the corners of the blankets and turning them under with severe military precision.

'You practically accused me of neglect!'

'You talk of neglect,' Sister Cooney hissed, 'and well you might. It wouldn't be the first time a patient died without medical attention because you were out on the golf course or otherwise unreachable, when you were supposed to be on call.'

'They'd have died anyway,' Doctor O'Connor-Crowley snapped.

129

'Oh, yes. They'd have died. But they had the right –'

'Don't you presume to lecture me, Sister.'

'I wouldn't waste my time.'

'You're being insubordinate.'

'You began this argument, you know.'

'And I'll finish it!' Doctor O'Connor-Crowley stormed out, tying her stethoscope into an inextricable knot as she went.

'What's wrong with her?' Nurse Lambert asked.

'She's afraid she may have given the Commander too much air.'

'Afraid? You'd never think it by her!'

'If she was sure of herself, she'd have no need to shout.'

'She's always giving too much air. I hear the patients complaining.'

'We'll have to check and see what he got,' Sister Cooney said. 'Doctor Staples was in the process of taking him off refills.'

'Poor man, will he be all right?'

'I don't know. I wonder, now,' she mused quietly, 'where he has the bottle?'

She reached in under the blankets near his leg and felt about. When she withdrew her hand, it held a flat bottle with about an inch of brandy still in it.

'Are you going to take it?' Nurse Lambert asked.

Sister Cooney shook her head and smiled. She reached in again under the blankets and settled the bottle beside the Commander's leg. 'It's all he's got. What harm can it do him at this stage?'

Later, word was sent to Mrs Barnwell and she came and sat beside him, a lank, drooping figure. Sister Cooney took her in a cup of tea and it steamed away on the locker until it filmed over and grew cold.

'It's no good!' Arty tossed Madeleine's letter aside petulantly. 'All the fun has gone out of it. We used write about every sort of daft thing. But now all we seem to write about is how funny it was deceiving each other like that. There's no surprise in it – and no romance either.'

'That's a lot of rubbish,' Vincent said. 'She's a real girl to you now – not just some silly moonstruck cow. What do you think romance is anyhow? The only worthwhile romance is reality.'

'Are you crazy!' Arty sat up, the very hairs on his head seeming to join in his incredulity. He waved his hand all round. 'There's reality for you – Phil there, and you, and all of us, stretched on our backs with the bleeding Con. What's romantic about that, tell me?'

'I was talking about fellows and girls,' Vincent said.

'Well, supposing you were, it's still just as crazy. Take yourself and Lily. She'll be going to Seapark soon, won't she?'

'I suppose she will,' Vincent conceded, his smile fading.

'There's reality for you,' Arty said, 'and there isn't much romance in it, is there?'

'God, Arty,' Vincent protested, feeling suddenly troubled and vulnerable, 'can't you talk about something cheerful?'

'That's the whole point of my argument,' Arty said triumphantly. 'There's nothing cheerful, nothing romantic, in reality. It's the dullest, most painful, most miserable thing I can think of.'

'Maybe you're right,' Vincent conceded.

'Of course I'm right!'

But Vincent felt that it wasn't as simple as that. There was a great deal more to be said for reality than had yet been said. Reality, he acknowledged, had two faces and one of them was harsh and cruel. But fantasy had no face at all. It was the mask covering a sore. To choose it was to opt out of life, to rush down a cul-de-sac with eyes closed. Lily was real. Their feeling for each other was real. The potential for happiness, or pain, in their relationship was real. The pain was inherent in the happiness, and in that lay the dangerous cutting edge of reality. But, if a man were to live with any kind of dignity, he had no choice. Acceptance of reality was a necessary kind of heroism.

'Well,' Arty was asking, 'what am I going to say to her this time?'

'Why ask me, when you won't listen to my advice?'

'Aw, Vincent, come on. Give us a hand.'

'Tell her the truth about yourself, then.'

'Tell her I've one wonky lung and they won't even put me on refills? Is that what you want me to tell her?'

'Why not! It's the truth, isn't it?'

'I think I'll pack it in altogether.'

'Tell her that, then.'

'How can I!'

'Just say, "Dear Madeleine, this is the end. Goodbye!"'

'I can't,' Arty said. 'I can't!' He looked at Vincent speculatively. 'Listen, Vincent, would you write it for me?'

'No!' Vincent shook his head vigorously. 'Never again!'

15

Eileen was dead.

Her body lay at the rest in the chapel downstairs, the light filtering in through lancet windows on her oak coffin and the dark-stained, hand-carved pews. They had taken him down in the lift and he had stood there looking at her face, peaceful and still. He had stooped to kiss her cold cheek and smelt in the hollow of her neck the waxen odour of death. Her features, serene, composed, invested mortality with mystery and beauty.

Later, he stood there again and watched his mother's tears. His father, gaunt and grey, supported her with strong, clay-hardened hands, his face set in bleak endurance. Their grief sharpened his guilt. It was he who should be lying there and not Eileen.

He had known for some time that it was inevitable. Sister Cooney had been the first to hint it to him. After his last visit, he had gone to her and begged to be told the truth.

'I'll ask Doctor Staples for you.'

'The truth is what I want – nothing else.'

'The truth is sometimes hard to accept,' Sister Cooney had said, her sharp face kindly and concerned.

Later, when she had consulted Doctor Staples, she returned,

looking grave. 'All I can tell you at the moment is that she is on the danger list. You were on it yourself once.' She looked at him hesitantly. 'You know there are different forms of this disease?'

'Oh,' he said apprehensively. 'What form has Eileen?'

'The name wouldn't mean anything to you.'

'I'd like to know it, all the same,' he said, as if the knowledge could somehow enable him to come to grips with it and defeat it.

'Acute miliary tuberculosis.'

It had been a simple matter after that to slip down to Mike Quinn, who was an acknowledged authority on all aspects of the disease by virtue of his ownership of one book, and borrow his *Encyclopaedia of Human Ailments*. Back in bed he found the relevant passage:

> Acute Miliary Tuberculosis is the most virulent form of this disease. Spreading by the blood, the bacilli become established in every part of the body and thus overcome the patient, not so much by the local damage as by the great general toxaemia, which produces symptoms not unlike those of typhoid fever – irregular fever, rapid pulse, dry skin and all the evidence of a raging pyrexia, leading to delirium and coma, followed almost inevitably by a fatal termination.

He saw her alive just once more. About eight o'clock in the evening he was summoned to her bedside.

'She's been calling for you,' Sister Duggan told him.

He found her lying with a cold compress on her forehead, the pupils of her eyes strangely dilated. They seemed to look through and beyond him and to focus – if they focused at all – on something infinitely remote. The fingers of her left hand, which lay outside the clothes, picked compulsively at the blankets.

134

When he took her hand in his, it was flabby, soft and tremulous. Sometimes her lips moved and she muttered something in a low tone.

He spoke her name and bent over to listen. Her head turned slightly towards him and she fixed him with that blind, unblinking stare.

'Eileen,' he called.

Her lips moved, but she made no sound that he could hear.

'Eileen,' he said again. 'Do you hear me?'

'Richard ... ' The words came faintly. 'Where's Richard?'

'I'm here, Eileen,' he said.

Her head turned away and she began to mutter incoherently.

'She's been like that most of the afternoon,' Sister Duggan, who was standing by at the foot of the bed, told him. 'Father Furlong came a while ago and anointed her. She's been a little easier since. But she keeps asking for you.'

He sat looking at her, with the numbed conviction that she was dying. It seemed to him that the essential Eileen had already receded from her eyes. There was no recognition in them, no awareness.

She began to mutter again and he leaned forward to listen. Amongst the jumble of words, he distinguished his own name and the word 'home'.

'Eileen,' he said, 'I'm here.'

She turned languidly towards the sound and spoke very distinctly. 'It's late, Richard. We'll have to be going home.'

'Yes,' he said and pressed her hand, 'we'll go soon.'

It was an exchange they had had a hundred times during childhood at the end of some day's adventure in remote fields. Twilight and mystery were woven into the words – along with fear and a reluctance to accept the inevitable.

They were the last words they spoke to each other. Almost

135

immediately she lapsed into inertia and lay there, as if asleep, but with her eyes open and staring.

'She seems easier now,' Sister Duggan said, as she gestured to him to withdraw.

In the morning, Matron, a large, comforting presence in navy blue, came with Sister Cooney to speak to him. 'You must prepare yourself for bad news,' she told him.

'Is she dead?' he asked bluntly.

'She's in a deep coma,' Matron said. 'We don't think she can recover.'

'She's tranquil,' Sister Cooney said. 'She's in no pain.'

'How long … ?'

'It's impossible to say – not very long.'

Eileen lingered on through the morning and the brown September afternoon, her life twirling like a hectic-stricken leaf on a thin stem. It was evening and the corridor was loud with the homely rattle of teacups when Sister Cooney came to tell him she was dead.

Now they were gathered in the chapel for her final journey home. The coffin had been fastened down and lay on trestles, honey-coloured in the slanting light, awaiting its removal. The undertaker, a fat man with a bunch of keys hanging from the index finger of his right hand, stood whispering to his father and Michael. His mother, a crushed figure in black, sat beside him in a pew. On the other side of him sat Liam, bewildered and broken.

'She was so young,' his mother had whispered over and over again, until he wanted to shout at her to stop, 'so young, and all her life before her.'

They had stood about his bed, caught for a moment in a frieze of grief, all of them welded by tragedy into an awareness of their common flesh, their common loss.

136

'A few months ago she was in her full health and it was you we were worried about,' Michael cried.

The undertaker was looking at his watch. Death was his business and it had to be organised efficiently. Grief was the climate in which he worked and he had inured himself to it. On the whole it was a profitable venture. Nobody wanted to be mean at such a time. An undertaker's bill was paid and not questioned.

'She was always so ... alive!' his father said.

They had sifted minutely through the circumstances of her death. Always at the end, they took refuge in some single statement that they repeated again and again. It was a statement that summed up some private vision they had of her, the simple words swelling to become a vehicle for all their feelings about her.

Some friends and neighbours had come to accompany her home. They stood about deferentially at the back of the little chapel, not wishing to intrude on the privacy of the family's mourning. At a nod from his father, the undertaker beckoned towards a group of men who came forward with subdued eyes, eager to express their sympathy in the one manly way that was open to them. The undertaker selected four of them and they bent willingly to the coffin, easier in their minds about the embarrassments of grief, because now they had something they could do. They lifted her gently onto their shoulders and moved down the chapel.

'She was talking about the cherries,' he told Michael. 'It was the last thing she talked about.'

'You only have them a few years, after all,' his mother cried.

At the door, she embraced him in wordless grief. His father put his arm roughly about them both. 'I don't like leaving you here, son,' he said.

137

'Poor Richard!' his mother said. 'We're all forgetting about you.'

The fat undertaker had closed down the tailgate of the hearse and stood about on the gravel, twirling his keys. It was over an hour's journey home at the pace funerals travelled, and the coffin was due in the parish church at six. He looked at his watch again and wondered if it was time to intervene.

Matron and some of the nurses were standing by. They came forward again to shake hands and sympathise. Sister Duggan had Eileen's few belongings in a case and handed them to Liam.

'I was looking after her chickens for her until she came home,' Liam had cried in the chapel.

Michael took the case from him and led him away to the hired car.

'What are we going to do at all!' his mother cried, as his father led her after them.

'God is good,' his father said ritually. 'In spite of everything, God is good!'

As he looked at them walk away, something hard in him revolted and he cried inside himself: There is no God. There is no good. There's nothing but disease and decay and death. He watched their departure through a spreading mist, and when the last car had gone and the avenue was silent except for the long sigh of grass, he allowed himself to be taken back to his room.

Sounds from the corridor intruded on his grief. People still walked about and talked and laughed. They were eating, sleeping, defecating, or otherwise engaged in some momentous enterprise. Eileen was dead and it meant nothing to them at all. Like a herd of antelope, grazing indifferently while one of their number was being savaged by lions, they would go on, singing and clapping their hands and making a great noise against the darkness. Eileen was dead and it made no difference at all.

16

It was quiet when Vincent slipped out of bed. There was no sound except breathing and soft, nocturnal sighing from the darkness beyond the verandah. He had watched until the night nurse had left the office and now he was as sure as he could be that she had gone below for a meal.

Bulbs in pale globes lit the corridor at intervals, the light reflecting off shiny walls. When he passed the entry that led to the bathrooms and toilets, he became more circumspect. It would be hard to give a satisfactory explanation if he were found in that part of the house so late at night. He stood at the ornate head of the stairs and listened. There was no sound at all.

He tiptoed swiftly down the stairs, keeping close to the wall. When he came to the bottom, he stood again and listened. Then he put his head out slowly and looked up the corridor. There was no one in the office. He was about to step across to the darkness of the recess and Lily's room when he heard footsteps and the sound of voices below him in the tiled entrance hall. He recognised the loud bray of Doctor O'Connor-Crowley. She was grumbling about being called out at such a late hour. Whoever was with her was explaining that it was an emergency. He stood listening as they crossed the hall and waited for the sound of the lift gates closing. But instead, he heard them begin the ascent of the stairs. He daren't go back or they would see him.

He heard his name whispered from the recess and stepped lightly across into the gloom. A hand caught his and drew him quietly into the room. They stood in the darkness behind the open door and listened to the footsteps. Vincent felt his heartbeat quicken, and tightened his grip on Lily's hand. They stood there, breathless, as the steps came nearer, stopped for a moment outside then turned up the corridor.

'That was a near thing,' Vincent whispered.

They listened as the sound receded – not moving, thrilled by the danger of discovery and by their nearness. They laughed a little hysterically, and whispered to each other to be quiet and then laughed again, drunk with the joy of touching hands and the scent of their bodies in the dark.

'I told you we'd meet in spite of them,' Vincent said.

It was the eve of Lily's departure to Seapark. Vincent had put in a request to visit her and had been refused. It was strictly forbidden for male patients to visit anyone except close relatives on the female floor.

'You'll have to wait now until she's gone,' Lily said.

'Close the door, then.'

'No. These doors are always kept open.'

They moved together in the friendly darkness, opening their arms to each other. It was something they had dreamed of many times. In their minds it had been prefaced with romantic dialogue and protestations of love. But now it seemed as natural as the confluence of two rivers and needed no words at all. Their bodies, meeting at many points, spoke of hunger and human need and deprivation.

'We'll meet again, Vincent, won't we?'

'Yes, of course, we will!'

'Sometimes I think we'll never see each other again.'

He pressed his face into her hair. It smelled fresh and newly washed, and curiously stamped with her youth, her beauty, her frail mortality.

A moist breath of autumn and ripeness came to them through the open window. There was a brittleness in the sound of wind through the trees that spoke of fall and ruin. Their ears, attuned to the corridor, caught the whisper of distant movement.

'It must be Elsie,' Lily said. 'Did you know she's back?'

'No,' Vincent said. 'When? How is she?'

'Yesterday. She had a haemorrhage just before she came in. I'm afraid she may be having another. She complained of spotting in the afternoon. That's probably why the doctor's here. She's a different Elsie – very down in herself.'

'God,' Vincent groaned, 'what hope is there for any of us!'

They clung together in silence, the dread of their disease and its mortal power oppressing them.

'Maybe the ones that die quickly are the lucky ones,' Vincent said with a surge of pessimism.

Outside they heard footsteps and voices on the corridor. Suddenly the light in the recess came on.

'My God!' Lily hissed. 'They're coming in here.'

She sprang guiltily away from Vincent, pushing him off balance. He stumbled backwards and struck a bed screen that crashed to the floor, bringing him with it. Lily screamed in fright. There was a rush of feet from outside. The room light came on and Nurse Bodkin and Doctor O'Connor-Crowley stood in the doorway.

Vincent picked himself up slowly and rubbed his ribs.

'What's the meaning of this?' Doctor O'Connor-Crowley rasped.

Vincent looked at Lily who was standing beside her bed, twisting the tassel of her dressing gown between her fingers and crying. His first feelings had been of shock and then fear. He was aware of the need to conciliate, to plead, to attempt to explain. But the sight of Lily's tears and the arrogant tone of the doctor's voice pushed him into truculence.

'It's not what you think ...' he began.

'Don't be insolent,' the doctor snapped. 'Get back to your floor and report to me in the office at twelve tomorrow.'

'Oh, no, Doctor, please,' Lily cried, as the threat to Vincent's future, inherent in the command, became clear to her.

The innocence of the encounter, and the sharp pitch of emotional stress to which it had brought him, were significant factors in Vincent's response. His voice, when he spoke, instead of being conciliatory, was angry.

'She's going away and we may never meet again. I came to say goodbye.'

'That's all ... we were doing,' Lily cried, 'saying goodbye.'

'At this hour of the night!' the doctor sneered.

'We asked for permission during the day and couldn't get it,' Vincent protested.

'You know the rules as well as I do.'

'Rules!' Vincent shouted, casting off all restraint, 'I'm sick of your rules! We may never see one another again, but nobody cares, because there's no provision for it in the rules. We may die and no one here will worry too much – as long as we do it according to the rules!'

Lily covered her face with her hands and began to sob. Nurse Bodkin bustled over to her and put her arm around her shoulder, making soothing noises and easing her into a sitting position on the bed.

'That's quite enough,' Doctor O'Connor-Crowley shouted.

143

'Get back to your floor at once. I shall deal with you in the morning.'

Vincent looked towards Lily, who raised her eyes and looked back at him sadly. Her mind was full of fears about his future. What decisions, made arbitrarily and in anger, would be handed down to him in the morning? What would happen to him if he were sent packing?

With his head lowered, Vincent walked out and padded heavily up the stairs. He stood on the verandah in his own ward and stared out into the darkness. Underneath, someone was awake and coughing. The lights of a car came probing around the corner of the building, cutting a wide swathe through the blackness and disappearing like a will-o'-the-wisp through the trees.

In bed, his mind kept turning in an endless loop, living and re-living what had happened. When the night nurse came and flashed her light curiously over him, he pretended to be asleep. He was surprised eventually by the cold greyness of morning, and sat up, despairing of rest. As soon as it was bright enough, he took out notepaper and wrote two letters – one to Arty and one to Lily. Then he retrieved his clothes and suitcase from the locker-room, dressed himself and packed his case.

Arty was still asleep, one arm hanging loosely over the side. Vincent resisted the temptation to wake him and tell him everything. He simply put the letters on Arty's locker and turned away.

It was seven and the night nurse had already begun her round at the other side of the house when he slipped downstairs. Lily's door was still open. It was not easy to pass without looking in. But it was best to leave her undisturbed. Arty would see that she got his letter before she left for Seapark.

Breakfast was being prepared in the kitchens. He smelled

144

frying bacon and heard the chatter of women as he walked across the tiled hall and let himself out through a side door.

The morning air was sharp and bracing as he turned down the avenue. He walked a little uncertainly, unused to the solid earth under his feet. The smells from the grass and the hedges were strange and fresh and exciting. When he turned to look, it seemed to him that the hospital was moving away from him like a phantom ship, butting through the September mists.

17

Since the interview in Matron's office, Sister Cooney and Doctor O'Connor-Crowley had barely been on speaking terms. Doctor Staples, in his brisk way, had dealt with the matter summarily and to the full satisfaction of neither.

'In so far as the patient was being phased off this treatment,' he had begun, pointing with the back of his pen to certain entries on Commander Barnwell's chart, 'it would be technically correct to say that there has been a minor error.'

Minor! Sister Cooney seethed silently under her blotched skin. How minor would it have been if the poor man had died?

Error! Doctor O'Connor-Crowley rolled the offensive word down the corrosive reaches of her mind. She did not make errors.

'What error?' she asked truculently.

'The patient received the same amount of air as he was given the previous week. Phasing out required a gradual reduction – at least 100 ccs less,' Doctor Staples said.

'That was my point entirely,' Sister Cooney said. She could not – and did not try to – hide the triumph in her voice at being thus vindicated.

'On the other hand,' Doctor Staples said, 'it would be

unscientific to assume that this had anything to do with his lung collapse. "*Post hoc – propter hoc*" is bad logic.'

'Precisely!' Doctor O'Connor-Crowley said. 'He already had had similar amounts – and more, much more – and nothing had happened.'

Doctors! Sister Cooney sneered to herself. Covering up for each other as usual -- 'dog does not eat dog', their sole code of ethics. 'There was an error,' she insisted.

'There were several errors,' Doctor Staples said, 'and one of them was this unseemly wrangle in front of the patient.'

'He was barely conscious,' Doctor O'Connor-Crowley said.

'All the more reason why he should have been having the full attention of you both,' Doctor Staples said sharply.

'I dislike incompetence,' Sister Cooney told the room in general, 'wherever – and in whoever – I find it.'

'Ladies!' Doctor Staples had an edge of impatience in his voice. 'I'm afraid I find you both culpable in this. As the patient is now out of danger, I don't propose to take the matter any further. You may consider the incident closed.'

'Of course the old rip was negligent,' he conceded to Sister Cooney later. 'I know all about her and her refills – 100 ccs more or less mean nothing to her. She might as well be pumping a bicycle!'

'Sister Cooney is inclined to exceed her authority,' he allowed carefully to Doctor O'Connor-Crowley when they were alone. 'She's a stickler for accuracy. We all have to keep on our toes when she's around.'

'Impossible woman!' Doctor O'Connor-Crowley complained.

'I suspect her trouble is menopausal,' Doctor Staples confided, smiling inwardly at his own two-faced diplomacy.

A melancholy came over Arty when Vincent left. He began to

grow morose. He sat for hours staring into a hand mirror, tilting it this way and that and bending his head. He took to long fits of massaging, until his scalp glowed a wealed pink and his arms dropped from exhaustion. His concern began to spread from his hair to his skin. He examined it for blotches and blemishes, and subjected any irregularities to the most rigorous scrutiny.

'Did you know,' he asked Phil, who had been trying to solicit his help all morning in the writing of a very important letter, 'that cancer can start as a little discoloration – even a tiny wart or mole?'

'Is that a fact?' Phil showed a diplomatic interest in the hope of gaining Arty's favour.

'It's like a time bomb you carry round with you,' Arty said, 'and the alarm mightn't go off for twenty-five years.'

'Is that a fact, now?' Phil said again.

'And it might go off tomorrow!' Arty examined a freckle on his nose with deep suspicion.

'Isn't it a wonder, now,' said Phil, seizing the chance to turn the conversation his way, 'that shaggin' chancer of a Dagg from Belfast didn't claim his dirty water could cure cancer too!'

'Did it do you no good at all?'

'No more nor if it was duck's piss!'

'Piss is supposed to be good for warts,' Arty said. 'Did you ever hear that?'

'No,' Phil said. 'Listen, Arty, I'm writing to this Dagg fellow. Would you –'

'Some warts are cancerous,' Arty said, laying the mirror aside and getting out of bed.

'Would you tell me what to say to him?'

'You're only wasting a stamp, Phil. You'll never get your money back.'

'God, Arty, you promised to help us!'

'Tell him it made your mickey fall off and you'll sue him for loss of your wife's affection,' Arty shrugged indifferently, as he drew on his dressing gown and headed for the bathroom, where there was a larger mirror.

'Christ, Arty, watch your language!'

'Wrap up a sausage and send it to him for proof,' Arty called as the door swung to behind him.

'You're a terrible man altogether!' Phil complained, mourning the ending of a conversation that had begun to interest him.

The ambulance that took Lily away brought Frank back. It was a shrunken Frank, whose body seemed to have contracted out of sympathy with his shrivelled spirit. He lay, propped up by pillows, his face a slaty waste of sagging flesh, with lines of tension around the mouth and dull eyes. A long bandage was fixed to the bottom of the bed and he was encouraged and bullied to pull on this several times a day, and hoist himself forward and perform exercises to rebuild the muscles of his butchered back.

After a few feeble and dispirited attempts to rotate his shoulders in a circular movement, or raise and lower his arms, he subsided with a groan and lay slumped until the nurse helped him up again and the torture continued.

'You must keep trying, Mr O'Shea,' Nurse Bodkin urged.

'What difference does it make?' Frank looked at her out of his sunken eyes.

'That's what you say now,' Nurse Bodkin said briskly, guiding his fumbling, unmotivated fingers towards the bandage. 'But what will you be saying if you see yourself in a month's time with a list on you like the Leaning Tower of Pisa? What will Mrs O'Shea say?'

What would Kitty say? He knew well what Kitty would say. Though it wouldn't make the least bit of difference to her what way he looked, she would not let the occasion pass without punishing him sharply for still being alive. She would survey him coldly with eyes that spat venom – Look at you with the gimp of an old scarecrow on you, they would say. A fine thing you're going to be to warm a woman's bed at night.

Her voice might be saying something different but that, in essence, would be the message. Kitty had that facility for slipping the knife in, even when on the surface she might only be talking about the weather. He wondered what she was doing at that very moment. It was something he seemed to have spent a great deal of his life wondering. Into his twilight existence her face floated like a mirage. He saw her coarsening features through the bottom and sides of a raised glass. He saw her eager body arched to welcome some casual stranger, her passion loosed in that spendthrift laugh that would never ring for him again.

'Why the hell didn't I die and be done with it!' Frank said bitterly.

'Mr O'Shea feels very sorry for himself. It's not like him at all,' Nurse Bodkin reported.

'It's a touch of postoperative melancholy,' Sister Cooney said. 'We'll have to snap him out of it and keep him to the exercises or he'll ruin himself.'

She closed the manila folder she was working on, and with a firm set to her finely whelked face, she strode to his bed. 'Mr O'Shea,' she said sternly, 'you haven't been doing your exercises properly.'

'What's the use, Sister,' Frank said listlessly.

'It's not yourself I'm worried about.' Her voice was harsh. 'It's the others. Think of the bad example you are to anyone on the list for surgery. What hope can they have, if they see you slumping about like a filleted herring, wallowing in self-pity? I'm ashamed of you. A man in your position should be giving a lead.'

'The poor schoolmaster must live his life in a glass cage and do nothing that would scandalise the parish!' Frank grumbled.

'That's more like it,' Sister Cooney eased her face into the makings of a smile. 'I'm glad to see there's some spirit left in you still.'

'Damn little, then!' Frank said.

'Come on, now,' Sister Cooney urged. 'Try stretching down to touch your toes. That's a good one to build up the muscles.' She stood at the bottom of the bed and reached out her hands to catch his and pull them forward.

'God!' Frank groaned, as she relaxed her grip and eased him back. 'It's like being on the rack.'

'It gets easier as you go on,' she encouraged. 'Try again.'

'I couldn't.'

'You must,' she insisted, taking his hands.

'Don't pull me,' Frank pleaded. 'I'll do it myself – if you'll give me time.'

He lifted his hands feebly and, leaning forward, dropped them languidly on the blanket in front of him. His body followed his hands a little, pushing them forward, until his head slumped down and he lay there, breathing laboriously.

From the bottom of the bed Sister Cooney eyed the limp hair on his thinning crown. 'Good!' she said. 'Now, try again – only put more effort into it this time.'

Frank fumbled for the bandage, caught it and eased himself cautiously back into a sitting position. She stood beside him, pressing his back down as he leaned forward again.

'Good!' she said. 'You didn't die yet.'

'No such luck!' Frank groaned.

'It gets easier with practice,' Sister Cooney said. 'Now, hold your two hands forward in front of you like this, as if you were going to dive. Then put as much of a stretch on them

151

as you can and move them apart and backwards, as if you were swimming.'

She stood and watched his weak attempts to comply. 'Back,' she directed, 'further back – much further back – back until you can't go any further, until you feel your chest is going to split in two.'

Frank dropped his hands and would have fallen, had she not steadied him and guided his fingers back to the bandage.

'A little rest,' she said briskly, 'and then we'll try again.'

'If this old body has anything to try with,' Frank gasped. 'Do you know what I feel like? I feel like a maggot in a carcass. I know I'm alive. But everything around me is dead.'

'The body is tougher than you think,' Sister Cooney said. 'It needs driving, that's all. It's a sophisticated kind of machine and, like a machine, you can't afford to let it get rusty or it'll seize up.'

'God!' Frank protested. 'If this thing of mine is a machine, it certainly needs oiling.'

'That's what I'm trying to tell you.' Sister Cooney smiled. 'Come on, now. We'll try a few more.'

'The tinnitus you can expect, I'm afraid,' Doctor Staples said, 'and the vertigo too – a little deafness even. Have you felt any deafness?'

'I don't think so,' Richard said.

'Well, you may have a little. All these are side effects of the streptomycin. So don't be too worried. Is the ringing in the ears bad?'

'Disconcerting more than anything else,' Richard said, hearing, even as he spoke, the tiny tintinnabulation, faint as fairy bells.

'And the PAS, of course, brings on nausea and discourages eating?'

152

'Yes – especially in the morning.'

Every morning since the new treatment had started he had been wakened to the thermometer and a medicine glass, half-full of a yellow, foul-tasting mixture that curdled in his stomach and sat there all day in a poisonous knot, waiting for the smell and taste of food to release its venom again.

'You're not having a very happy time, are you?' Doctor Staples said.

'I'm not complaining,' Richard hurried to assure him. 'I just thought that … as it's new … you'd like to know …'

'Everything! Absolutely everything!' Doctor Staples said. 'No detail is too small. As a matter of fact, I'm preparing a paper on the side effects for the medical association at this very moment. The treatment is prolonged. You understand that?'

'I wasn't expecting any instant miracles,' Richard smiled.

'The prognosis is quite good, though – very encouraging, in fact,' Doctor Staples said.

Anything, Richard thought, would be better than sawing half a man's chest away. He had seen Frank's mutilated back when they had both been down for screening, and had been deeply shocked. There was dignity, at least, in the way Eileen had died. Thank God she had been spared the ordeal of surgery.

It was the first time since her death that he had been able to think of it with anything like acceptance. There had been long weeks when he lay sunk in gloom and introspection. During the rest hours and at night, he had turned his face to the wall and cried over their shared youth and all the bonds of sun and blowing grass and long evenings full of the sound of tumbling rooks that tied their lives together.

Occasionally he had gone in to sit by Commander Barnwell's bed and seek comfort in his sea-scoured face and calm eyes.

'Dreadfully sorry, old chap!' the Commander had said

when he first heard, his voice wheezing and whistling in his throat.

Richard had nodded his head and looked at the floor and said nothing.

'It was so untimely,' the Commander said passionately after a long silence, 'so very untimely.'

Richard nodded again, and again there was silence.

'Must come for all of us one day.' The Commander stirred fretfully in bed and rearranged the blankets. His breath, after the exertion, came in startled gasps. 'What's life,' he said with a pessimism that fed Richard's gloom, 'only waiting for the end.'

18

Arty's melancholy had deepened. He sat with his hand mirror all day and every day. He bent and twisted himself before it, jerking suddenly this way and that, as if he were lying in wait for disease, determined to pounce on it before it could strike. He pestered anyone who came along to look at his back and examine it for spots. The other patients began to avoid him, to look at him oddly, to wonder about him.

One morning after breakfast and a prolonged peering into the mirror, Arty broke and screamed at Phil, who had come across to borrow a newspaper. 'Keep away from me, Phil! Keep away! It's contagious.'

'God bless us and save us!' Phil exclaimed in alarm, 'What's wrong, Arty, boy?'

'Smallpox!' Arty cried.

Phil looked at him queerly and began to back off. 'Keep your old paper,' he said defensively. He turned away, and when he had got a safe distance, he began to whistle – a moist whistle that said he wasn't really disturbed at all about Arty's strange behaviour.

'Here's the bleedin' paper!' Arty flung it across to him. 'Only keep away!'

'I think I'll go across and have a chat with that young fellow who came in the other day,' Phil said in a conversational tone to no one in particular and rushed out to Sister Cooney's office. 'God, Sister,' he poked his head around the jamb of the door, 'that Arty fellow is acting terrible strange. He says he has some disease.'

'Isn't he in the right place for it?' Sister Cooney smiled and looked up at the board in front of her as the bell rang. 'There's somebody ringing in your ward now. Maybe it's him.'

'That fellow do have forty different diseases a day lately,' Phil said. 'You never know with him whether he's coddin' or in earnest. I don't think he knows himself sometimes.'

Sister Cooney pressed a button on the panel and stood up. 'We'll soon find out,' she said briskly.

'He do be usin' cruel bad language lately too,' Phil complained piously.

She shooed him back to bed in front of her and he went meekly enough, entering with studied indifference, tapping his fingertips together as he went. He threw his dressing gown casually on the chair and – with never a glance at Arty – jumped between the sheets, picked up the newspaper from the floor beside the bed, opened it out and peered over the top, his ears tuned to the conversation.

'Well, Arty. Something wrong?' Sister Cooney asked.

'Smallpox, look!' Arty pointed his finger to his open mouth.

'Listen, Arty Byrne,' Sister Cooney said crossly, 'I've no time for joking. What's wrong with your mouth?'

'Looh ah ih!' Arty's voice thickened and blurred into animal grunts as he tried to speak and extend his tongue at the same time.

Sister Cooney examined his tongue critically. 'There's nothing the matter with your tongue. It's perfectly normal.'

'Spos – uk!' Arty said.

'Draw in your tongue and speak normally.'

'I said look at the spots.'

'There are no spots.'

'There are – hundreds of them. I've been watching them multiply all morning. My tongue is covered with them – uk.'

'Put in your tongue,' Sister Cooney ordered.

'It's smallpox. You'll have to isolate me,' Arty told her.

'Smallpox!' Sister Cooney's voice was scathing. 'Do you know what smallpox is? If you had smallpox, you'd have a rash. Let's see your chest and abdomen.' Briskly she unbuttoned his pyjama top and examined him. 'Not a trace. Not a thing.'

'That's what I'm trying to tell you,' Arty said, with a touch of desperation in his voice. 'The rash is on my tongue.'

'You can't have a rash on your tongue.'

'But I have – uk!' Arty said again.

'Keep in your tongue, please.'

Arty closed his mouth and began to brush the heel of his open hand against his left temple in a repeated gesture of frustration. Sister Cooney was surprised to see tears in his eyes.

'I knew you wouldn't believe me,' he said.

'If it makes you feel any better, I'll get the doctor to have a look at you when he comes.'

As soon as she had gone Phil was out of bed again and, with a half-fearful look at Arty, put on his dressing gown and sauntered out to spread the news. 'That Byrne fellow is gone loony,' he told whoever would listen to him. 'And it wasn't today or yesterday he began either, if you ask me. Did I ever tell you about the letters he used write to ones he didn't know from Adam – mad letters about him being an airplane pilot? God, you meet all kinds in a place like this!'

When Doctor Staples came, he examined Arty and listened patiently to his self-diagnosis. The doctor neither confirmed nor denied that he was suffering from smallpox – which pleased Arty immensely. 'Yes,' he agreed, 'I think we should shift you. We'll move you to a room of your own – put you under observation. Would you like that?'

'Yes,' Arty said. 'I think it would be safer.'

'Tell me this,' Doctor Staples asked, 'you've been depressed lately, am I right?'

'Yes,' Arty said, feeling that at last he had someone who understood him and was taking his case seriously.

'Well, we can do something about that straightaway and at the same time keep you under observation. How would that suit you?'

'Fine!' Arty was relieved.

When a week passed and Arty's condition had not improved, Doctor Staples returned with a worried frown. 'We may have to send you out to … another hospital … for some treatment. You wouldn't mind that, would you? You'd go out in the morning and be back again in the afternoon.'

'What hospital?' Arty asked.

'We'll have to arrange about that,' Doctor Staples said vaguely.

'Get in touch with Hearne,' he told Sister Cooney, when they were back in the office. I think a course of electroconvulsive therapy is what young Byrne needs.'

'The mental hospital?' Sister Cooney looked concerned.

'Yes, but don't tell him that – not for the moment, anyway.'

'Poor fellow!' Sister Cooney said. 'He's normally in such high spirits.'

'That's a characteristic of manic-depressive psychosis, isn't it?' Doctor Staples said. 'Periods of elation followed by bouts of depression. Delusions of physical disease are common in the

158

depressive part of the cycle. We'll just have to see what a course of ECT will do for him.'

The following morning, Arty was taken by ambulance to the huge Victorian red-brick pile on the edge of town – a massive structure set well back in the fields and surrounded by a high wall to protect the sensibilities of the sane from too close a confrontation with one of society's more disagreeable problems.

He was brought back a few hours later, dazed and dreamy, with a dull headache and no very clear notion of what had been done to him or why. All he remembered was being strapped to a couch, the sudden fear, the cold touch of electrodes to his head, and the convulsive shock before the blackout.

Elsie Hogan, her young face wasted and gaunt, was lying in bed reading a letter. She was in a ward with strangers now. Lily was gone. Mrs Doran was gone too, slipping off one wet October day with her husband, her eyes – even as she said goodbye – filled with the anticipation of familiar fields and deep pastoral quiet. Elsie had wept for kind Mrs Doran and for her husband, that strange, silent, sympathetic man, lifting his feet cautiously as he sidled across the polished floor. There was something strong and elemental in them that would outlast a world in flux.

The letter was from Lily, in neat, sloped handwriting, like careful embroidery.

It's all different here. Everyone's on the ground floor in chalets – wooden chalets in fields of grass. The atmosphere is different too. There's more hope here. In Ardeevan we just lay and rotted and nothing ever happened between Doctor Staples's weekly rounds – except that someone died. A lot of people are on streptomycin now and there are new operations. Did I tell you I may have to have surgery?

Elsie let the letter drop and sighed. It was the atmosphere that

159

was killing. No one ever knew what was to happen next, as Lily said. The place was full of rumours and gloomy talk, most of it ignorant and ill-informed. She felt herself drowning in disease, like the fly she once found floundering in the filth of her sputum mug.

> Vincent came to see me and stayed all day. He looked very well and was full of talk of making his way in the world and starting a business some day. He's in England now – a place called Warwick. He's got a job in a factory. He's saving three pounds a week and putting it in the post office at home. He writes every week without fail. Do you remember how you were on to me to write to him? No need for that anymore ...

Elsie put away the letter and cried. She did not know why she was crying. It wasn't like her at all.

A flurry again in Commander Barnwell's room. A running and ringing in the darkening afternoon, urgent voices on the phone and the grind and clang of the lift as it came and went.

Next door, Richard heard and wondered. Something heavy and metallic was wheeled in. Oxygen? Collapse again? Outside on the corridor, the rumours were beginning to spread. His heart – his other lung – both lungs – the poor man was having a haemorrhage. His door was closed. That was a bad sign.

When the doctor had come and gone and the place was quiet again, Richard put on his dressing gown and tiptoed across. There was no response to his quiet knock. He opened the door and looked in. The screens were around the bed and the draught from the door set them billowing like sails. In the half light, he had the odd notion that the Commander was afloat on a full and soundless tide. He stood uncertainly, listening, wondering if he should go any further or retreat before someone came along. There was a strange silence about the room that puzzled him. He coughed mildly to test its depth and the sound was spirited away and absorbed into the stillness.

'Commander,' he whispered and stepped forward towards the bed. The door snapped shut behind him. There was no sound, no movement from the bed. Outside, the wind whistled thinly along the fluted tiles and stirred the open window sash.

He pulled the cloth of the screens aside and peered into the dimness. The Commander was lying on his back. His head rested on the pillow at an unusual angle, the chin tilted abnormally high, so that, from the foot of the bed, Richard was looking into the dark pits of his nostrils. There was nobody with him – and that was odd.

He was just drawing the screens apart to step inside, when the door opened. Sister Cooney came in and snapped on the light. Even as he turned in alarm, he carried with him, trapped on his retina, the picture of the Commander's face, hollow and empty.

'Richard! What are you doing here?'

He stared wordlessly at her, seeing only that pale, withdrawn face.

'You shouldn't be in here,' Sister Cooney said. There was compassion and no reprimand in her voice.

'The Commander!' he said in a shocked tone, whose grief took him unawares. 'He's dead, isn't he?'

'Back to your ward now, like a good fellow.' Sister Cooney took him by the arm and he went with her, unresisting.

'I was talking to him this morning,' he said. 'Look.' He pointed to his locker. 'He gave me that book.'

'You'd better get into bed.' Sister Cooney, noting the way he trembled, helped him off with his dressing gown and tucked him in.

'He is dead, isn't he?'

She nodded without speaking.

'He gave me that book only this morning – *Jane's Fighting Ships*. It lists every ship in the British Grand Fleet in the First World War.'

'I'll get you a warm drink and a hot-water bottle,' Sister Cooney said. 'The poor man had a seizure,' she continued, busying herself at the blankets. 'It was to be expected, you know. He never really recovered from that setback he had.'

'I was talking to him this morning,' Richard said again, wondering why he could not control his shivering. 'He was all right then.'

'It's a shock, I know,' Sister Cooney said.

'We were talking about the Battle of Jutland. He was showing me the ships that were lost in the battle. He was always talking about Jutland. He was there, you know.'

'It was the way he would have liked it,' Sister Cooney said. 'Quick in the end.'

'He was to go and live in Falmouth,' Richard said. 'He told me it was all fixed up. Mrs Barnwell … ' He stopped and looked at Sister Cooney. 'Does she know?'

'Not yet. We haven't contacted her yet.'

'She was coming this evening. He said she was coming.'

'Poor woman!' Sister Cooney said. 'She knew, of course. She was expecting this.'

He saw the Commander's pale face, the nose pinched and sharp, the eyes expressionless, like the windows of a deserted house. Was that what she was expecting?

When he had taken the tea and lay warmly wrapped and no longer shivering, Sister Cooney left him. He lay with his eyes closed, conscious of his own body, conscious of the body in the other room, and the difference now between them. He expected to die, but the expectation was always of something remote,

162

deferred. He wondered if the Commander had known, if Eileen had known. He found himself praying for Eileen and the Commander and all the dead, wherever they were. Death, whatever it was, was a reality, a more important reality than life, if one were to judge by its duration. Its mystery somehow diminished life, or did it enlarge it by making life and its purpose more mysterious still. It certainly did not diminish God or lessen His reality. In the face of such mystery, God was much more than just a protective wing to creep under.

Later, when Mrs Barnwell came, Sister Cooney took her in to see Richard. She extended her thin, cold hand and accepted his commiseration.

'He was always a free spirit,' she said. 'Clover Lodge didn't suit him at all. He felt landlocked in the middle of all those fields.'

'He talked of moving to Falmouth,' Richard said.

'Yes.' Mrs Barnwell turned momentarily away. 'It was all arranged.'

She shook his hand again before leaving and he lifted the book from the locker. 'I'd like to return this,' he said. 'It was his.'

'You keep it,' Mrs Barnwell said. 'Sister tells me you were his friend.'

'He was a good friend to me,' Richard said.

'Misfortune,' Mrs Barnwell said, 'makes friends of us all.'

'I don't see any great change in you,' Kitty O'Shea told her husband. 'You look much the same as you always looked.'

'How would you know?' Frank asked. 'You haven't really seen me for years.'

'You haven't been that long away.' Kitty smiled, wilfully misunderstanding him.

It was her smile that always did for him. It hinted at intimacies once shared and now denied. It stirred the man in him even as it gored him. It was a trap from which he could never escape.

'Or is it that it doesn't seem long?' he continued bitterly, knowing the futility of carping, but being unable to stop it. 'Why did you come at all?'

'To see my lord and master, what else!' she laughed.

'It's a long time since I was that – if I ever was.'

Frank's mind went back to that torrid summer when they had melted into intimacy. He had climbed through her window in the sweet nights, nights that would torment his memory for ever with the perfume of darkness and intrigue. Even then she had taken the initiative.

'You like me, don't you?' she had asked, her long hair loosened for sleep.

'You know I do.'

'Well, then, what are you worried about?'

After that he had worried about nothing at all. He had been a cheerful fellow in those days and life was as inconsequential as a laugh on the wind or the carelessly squandered words of a song. Her red hair was a beacon in the night – a flame in which he had long since been charred.

'Well, whose fault was that?' Kitty took up the challenge again.

'*Mea culpa!*' Frank said. '*Mea maxima culpa!*'

'Christ!' Kitty exclaimed in exasperation, 'Why do schoolmasters always have to talk like that? I often wonder if they're men at all.'

She looked at him in disgust. He would take that too, as he took all the rest. Why couldn't he rise up and assert himself, shout at her, curse her, take off a great belt with a brazen buckle on it, like some muscular labouring man and beat hell out of her? You could have respect for a man who lusted after you and fought for

164

you and took you. But none for this milksop, who backed away and threw little delicately-barbed darts and had such reliance on the supremacy of reason and words.

'Why do you come at all?' Frank asked. 'You haven't come all this way just to tell me you despise me, have you?'

'As a matter of fact,' Kitty said in a carefully careless tone, 'there is something you ought to know before that busybody Condon gets on to you about it.'

'Father Condon? About what?'

'You haven't had a visit – or a letter from him, then?'

'No. What's wrong? Are you in some kind of trouble? Don't tell me you're … '

'What kind of a fool do you think I am!' Kitty said impatiently. 'It's nothing like that.'

'What, then?'

'I can just see him looking down that long nose of his and saying in that sanctimonious voice: "There's something you ought to know, Mr O'Shea … "'

'What should I know?' Frank asked, his mind braced against shock.

'A lot of gossip! That's all it is,' Kitty said carelessly. 'People can never mind their own business.'

'What should I know?' Frank insisted.

Kitty took out her cigarettes and lit one nonchalantly. She drew in deeply and exhaled through her nose, then snapped the cigarette briskly from her mouth and pointed it at him with a flourish. 'You remember I had to get in a barman to help with drunks and keep a bit of law and order about the place?'

'I remember,' Frank said bleakly, with the familiar sensation of being sucked into a morass. 'Is it O'Gorman you're talking about?'

'Tom, yes.'

Her use of the Christian name angered him. She had never used his own for years – he was always 'you' or 'your man there'.

'Tom, Dick or Harry,' he said, 'what does it matter! So yourself and O'Gorman have been up to something? You don't expect me to be surprised, do you?'

'I knew you'd jump to conclusions,' Kitty said. 'Do you want me to tell you or not?'

'Better you than Father Condon, I suppose,' Frank said, staring at the blankets.

'It's not what you think, mind!'

'Nothing is ever what I think.'

'I – we – thought it a good idea at the time, with the late closing and it so hard to get people off the premises – and all the cleaning up to be done afterwards … '

'Thought what a good idea?'

'That he should live in.'

'A very good idea!' Frank said bitterly. 'So – convenient and everything.'

'Will you listen to me!' she hissed.

'Will *you* listen to me!' Frank raised his eyes angrily. 'There's been one thing understood between us for years and that was that you were to be discreet. You owe me that much – if nothing else. Never on the premises. That was our agreement.'

'You're getting it all wrong,' Kitty said. 'He's not that kind of fellow.'

'I hope he keeps his door locked at night, then, if he isn't,' Frank said venomously.

'As a matter of fact, he does.'

'I won't ask how you found out,' he taunted.

The locked door – if it was really true – made him feel more despondent than ever. It would intrigue and challenge her.

166

'You're just like old Condon,' she said, 'coming poking about in his sly way.'

'It's no business of mine, of course!' Frank said sarcastically.

'I soon put the run on that fellow,' Kitty continued without comment. ' "It's not right for a married woman to have a man in the house and he not her husband," he says. "It's a cause of scandal." "That makes two of us, Father," says I, thinking of that whey-faced housekeeper of his. "Haven't you a woman in the house that's not your wife!" ' She laughed in her careless way before drawing on her cigarette.

'For your own sake you should get rid of him – or make him live out,' Frank said quietly after a period of silence.

'Why the hell should I?'

'If you don't know yourself, there's no use in me telling you.'

'Bloody hypocrites, the lot!' Kitty said.

She crushed her cigarette in the ashtray and stood up to go. 'So, now you know,' she said.

She looked so competent and self-assured, so hard, so distant from his own thought and feeling that she might just as well have been a stranger, passing by without a glance in the street. The only thing that linked them was the embarrassing albatross of a marriage in whose death both of them had been guilty.

19

A Christmas tree had been set up in the corridor with fairy lights that winked on and off. There were balloons in all the wards and coloured paper that hung in drooping loops. The light came strangely rich through gaudy lanterns and shone on a brave display of Christmas cards.

On Christmas Eve a candle-lit procession, led by Matron, came to sing carols. The wind from the verandah set their long cloaks billowing and the candle flames aflutter. The sound, blown faint from distant wards, was melancholy with memories of other, happier Christmases.

On the day itself there was a special menu and paper hats were distributed. In the afternoon there was dancing on the wards. Beer, stout and a furtive drop of spirits were in circulation.

Sister Cooney watched the festivities develop with a benign eye. A sprig of holly with three berries was taped with sticking plaster to the wall over her desk. From time to time she glanced a little apprehensively at the numbered board with its blank bulbs. An emergency at a time like this could spoil everything. Looking in at the observation ward, with its partly screened beds, she hoped that Mike Quinn – poor man – wouldn't take it into his head to go in a hurry. Downstairs, too, there was young Elsie.

From Arty's room came the sound of an accordion. He was sitting on the side of the bed, his head slightly tilted, his eyes closed. His foot tapped the floor in time to the music. Ted Nugent leaned his shoulder against the doorjamb, looking in at him.

'Can't you play something a bit more lively?' Ted called.

Arty opened his eyes slowly and inclined his head towards a notice on the door – a notice he had put there himself. 'Can't you read?' he asked.

'KEEP OUT – SMALLPOX,' Ted read and laughed. 'You don't really believe that, do you?'

Arty closed his eyes again and concentrated on the music.

'Hey, it's Christmas!' Ted called, as he turned to leave. 'Can't you play something cheerful?'

'I can only play the way I feel,' Arty said.

Jack Carbery had put on his blue serge suit for the occasion and sat in the middle of a few friends, his collar stud gleaming, and the apple in his throat bobbing about like a cork on water as he drank. Jack was in a cheerful mood. He had a good roof over his head, clean sheets, enough to eat and a bottle of stout in his hand.

'Do you know what it is?' he enquired, wiping his mouth reflectively with the back of his hand. 'There's a power of good men gone since this time last year.'

'Ah,' said Joe Connors, a dark little man who reached forward with spatulate fingers for the corkscrew, 'there's only a few of us left.'

They began to make a head count, lingering over the names with relish, proud of being survivors. Carbery took a pack of cards out of his pocket and dealt them for Twenty-five. He tilted his head as he dealt, to keep the smoke that curled up from his cigarette out of his eyes. 'I suppose Mike out there will be the next to go,' he said in a pleasant conversational tone.

'Let him hould his hoult till the day is over, anyway,' Joe said. 'He have no business dyin' today and muckin' up everything.'

Phil sat on the side of Frank's bed and talked. 'That Arty have it cruel bad, whatever he have,' he said. 'I was down there to see him and he hardly spoke to me. He have a notice on his door. Do you know what it says?'

'I know,' Frank said wearily. 'I heard all about it.'

'But you haven't heard the worst. He says now it's typhoid he have and it's all my fault.'

'Your fault?' Frank began to show some interest.

'He says typhoid comes from pellucid water –'

'Polluted,' Frank suggested.

'Well, some kind of water, anyway. He's trying to make out that I gave it to him when I gave him a spoonful of that … stuff … I got from that shagger in Belfast. He says it was just dirty water and I poisoned him. Did you ever hear the like of that? No wonder they're sending him over to the mad house for th' electric.'

Frank looked at him sardonically. He didn't like what he saw. There wasn't much subtlety or human sympathy about Phil. He was an overgrown child who never saw beyond his own narrow world.

'Any fellow that'd pay a pound a bottle for dirty water – water that could very well carry typhoid,' Frank said severely, 'should have his head examined too. A touch of th' electric would do him no harm at all.'

Phil got up from the bed abruptly and turned away with an awkward gesture – his usual response when he felt insulted.

'You'd want to mind who you'd be talkin' to in this place,' he protested.

'You'd want to mind who you'd be taking the cure from, too,' Frank said.

Richard, wearing the new dressing gown and slippers that had been his mother's practical present, stood at the window, looking out over the bare countryside. The river, swollen and bloated, lay heavy on the sunken fields. Everything was stark and colourless – a predominance of mud and slate washes – just like his life.

'They're dancing up front. Why don't you come and join them?'

He turned to see Nurse Lambert smiling at the door. Her butterfly cap sat at a saucy angle on her black hair.

'Who am I to dance with?' He smiled back at her.

'Me!' She held out her hand in invitation.

'Aren't you on duty?'

'Who cares! It's Christmas.'

'So it is,' he said, his smile fading.

'Well, come on, then!'

He took her outstretched hand – very soft, very feminine – and allowed her to lead him away.

Out on the corridor, Nurse Bodkin was hovering hopefully near a suspended piece of mistletoe.

'Happy Christmas!' she called invitingly to Ted Nugent as he passed.

'God, Nurse,' Ted exclaimed virtuously, 'there's nothing for a hot-blooded sinner like me to do when he sees you coming, except close his eyes and pray for continence.'

'Go on out of that!' Nurse Bodkin crowed with delight. 'You men are all the same. A girl wouldn't be safe with one of you.'

'That's not our fault,' Ted said complacently. 'If your nature is fire, all you can do is burn.'

Nurse Bodkin pointed overhead and simpered. 'Aren't you going to honour the mistletoe?'

Ted made a loose grab at her before continuing on his way. When he was at a safe distance, he turned and called. 'You're a terrible woman altogether to be leading a fellow on like that! I'd better go before you tempt the two of us into dismantling and abusing the sacred structure of the Sixth Commandment.'

In the back ward a fiddle had struck up. Two or three couples began to dance. The rest sat and watched.

'More women is what we need,' the men cheered as Nurse Lambert and Richard walked in.

'It isn't safe to come in here.' Nurse Bodkin winked in delight as she waltzed past.

'Dance, Nurse, dance,' the men roared, surrounding Nurse Lambert, who was young and attractive and popular.

'Later,' she smiled and held out her arms to Richard.

He was disturbingly aware of her as they moved off. Her arms, which were bare to the elbows, were freckled and lightly downed in the artificial light. He began to wonder about her life outside the hospital.

'Do you like dancing, Nurse?' he asked.

'Yes, I do,' she said. 'And don't call me Nurse. My name is Keelan.'

'That's an unusual name.'

'It shouldn't be, then. It's Irish. *Caol* and *fionn* – slender and fair.'

'Well,' he said, eyeing her dark hair, 'it half suits you anyway.'

'Nobody's perfect,' she laughed.

As soon as the dance ended she was swept away by somebody else. Richard sat on a bed and watched her for several dances before claiming her again.

'I thought you were never going to rescue me,' she teased.

Just as the dance was finishing she drew him towards the door. 'Let's get out of here before the mob swamps us again.'

Richard opened the door and they slipped away. Their going was noticed and raucous cheers followed them.

Out on the corridor, Keelan took her stand under the mistletoe. 'Well, aren't you going to kiss me?'

Richard put his arms awkwardly about her and brushed her lips with his. 'Happy Christmas!' he said.

'Maybe it will be – yet!' she laughed and, taking his hand, led him into a storeroom and closed the door.

Sometime in the early evening a bell rang and there was a flurry about Mike Quinn's bed. Screens were pulled, lurching and swaying on screaming castors, the curtains swelling like sheets in a squall. Sister Cooney came, a calming influence, with a syringe in a kidney dish. Later she was seen phoning from the office. A nurse remained by the bed monitoring Mike's pulse.

An hour passed before there was another flurry, this time from the corridor. The voice of Doctor O'Connor-Crowley, like a racing-engine snarling through the gears, bore down on Sister Cooney, who sat writing in the office.

'Inconsiderate!' she roared. The office door shuddered behind her, and a baying, as of hounds savaging each other, filled the suddenly silent wards. Presently they erupted like twin explosions to examine Mike Quinn.

'This man is dying,' Doctor O'Connor-Crowley shouted. 'There's absolutely nothing that anyone can do.' She snapped the screens together as she emerged. The sound was as final as the closing of a coffin lid.

She looked down through the wards where the festive celebrations had momentarily stopped. On a sudden impulse she was

173

off, shouting as she went, 'What's going on here? Why aren't you people in bed? This is a hospital – not a hotel. Sister! Sister! Who gave these patients permission to have alcohol? Who authorised this? Back to your wards. Back to your beds. What, in God's name, has anyone here to celebrate?'

When everybody was suitably chastened and miserable, she left, cannonading down the corridor in great rolls of receding thunder. Near the stairhead she met Phil, who was emerging from a game of cards in one of the single rooms and had missed all the theatricals.

'A Happy Christmas, Ma'am,' Phil oozed – the day that was in it and a little whiskey fortifying his courage.

'What's happy about it, you stupid little man!' she cried. 'Don't you realise that it's the last Christmas most of you in here are ever likely to see?'

'Wasn't that a terrible thing to say to anyone?' Phil poured complaint into the receptive ear of Sister Cooney, as he sought comfort at her door.

'Don't mind that one,' she soothed. 'Here's a bit of news that'll cheer you up. Her tour of duty is almost done. She'll be leaving for good before the New Year. What do you think of that, now?'

'We'll celebrate for a week,' Phil exulted.

'We might even take longer!' Sister Cooney smiled. 'Happy Christmas, Phil!'

At tea-time the momentum of the day – or what was left of it after Doctor O'Connor-Crowley's intrusion – petered out and things began to sag. People sat about, replete and vacant. Ghosts of other Christmases began to walk and nudge.

Downstairs, Elsie Hogan, the bloom of youth scoured from her skeleton, lay waiting for the haemorrhage that would end it all. Her hair clung in damp strands to her forehead, emphasising

174

the whiteness of her face with the starkness of a black border on a mourning card.

Behind his screens, Mike Quinn gagged on ropes of his own phlegm, but was considerate enough to hang on a little longer. Everyone was asleep before the night nurse came on him, hunched and still, a smile on his wasted features in the soft halo of torchlight.

20

Frank looked up in surprise when Matron walked in. The morning was her usual time for coming, a flurry of nurses preceding her, squaring corners of blankets, clearing lockers, thumping pillows, crisp and antiseptic as they swept through. Then in their wake, a stately schooner under full sail – Sister Cooney bobbing like a fretful tug in attendance – she hove in sight, a strongly-timbered woman, solid and soundly ballasted.

'Someone to see you, Mr O'Shea,' Matron said, a concerned look on her face.

Frank sat up, a faint alarm bell ringing in his head. It would have to be some unusual visitor to be thus announced by Matron.

'Is anything wrong?' he enquired.

'Inspector O'Connell wishes to speak to you,' Matron said gently. 'I'm afraid you must prepare yourself for a shock. He has some very distressing news.'

'Kitty!' Frank exclaimed. 'What's happened?'

'Your wife has had … a very serious … accident,' Matron said hesitantly. She beckoned to someone outside and a garda inspector walked in.

'Where? How? How is she?' Frank raised himself laboriously in the bed, before subsiding weakly into the pillows.

'Perhaps,' the inspector said, when the introductions had been made, 'you would leave us, Matron. I think it might be easier on Mr O'Shea if I spoke to him alone.'

'Of course,' Matron said. 'Ring for Sister or myself if you need us.'

The inspector accompanied her to the door and closed it carefully after her. He laid his cap, containing his gloves, upside-down on the locker.

'What happened? Why are you here?' Frank asked.

'Your wife … ' the inspector began.

'Is she dead?'

The inspector looked at him keenly as he spoke, measuring his words, gauging the reaction. 'There was a fire …' he began.

'Oh my God!' Frank covered his face with his hands. The inspector's evasive reply was sufficient answer to his question.

'We did all we could,' the inspector said.

Frank began to shake his head violently. 'Not dead!' he said. 'She can't be dead!'

'I'm sorry to have to bring you this terrible news,' the inspector said. He turned away to face the window, a tall man with grizzled, close-cropped hair. There was silence in the room for some time as he waited for Frank to regain his composure, to ask the inevitable questions. The gutter beneath the window, he noticed, was half-choked with a black silt, the residue of dead leaves.

'How did it happen?' Frank asked at last.

'We're not sure. We think an oil heater may have overturned – or perhaps it was left too close to some curtains. It started in the bedroom. The fire brigade from town was on the scene within twenty minutes of the alarm and got it under control very quickly. But when we broke in, they were dead.'

'They?'

'O'Gorman, the bartender, and your wife. Smothered – the two of them.'

'The two of them ...' Frank echoed the words, then lay with his head sunk on his chest, a man in a stupor.

Silence again in the room, a long, agonising silence.

'Would you like me to call someone?' the inspector enquired, looking at him anxiously.

'Smothered, you say?'

'Mercifully, yes. The fire hadn't touched them at all.'

'Who raised the alarm?'

'One of our men on patrol. He noticed the flames and the smoke.'

The inspector coughed apologetically and placed his hands together, uncertain how best to say what had to be said next.

'There's ... something ... else,' he began slowly.

Frank lifted his head and looked at him, waiting for him to continue.

' ... something you should know.'

'Yes?'

'The ... ah ... manner in which they were found would seem to indicate that both had been drinking heavily. There were a number of bottles and glasses in the room. The doctor found a very high alcohol content in their blood.'

'Oh, God!' Frank moaned.

The inspector looked at his sunken head with compassion. It was a distressing part of his duty to have to tell people things they were better off without hearing. 'They died in their sleep,' he said.

'There's something you're leaving out,' Frank said suddenly in a harsh tone. 'Isn't there?'

The inspector sighed with relief. He had been wondering if the man suspected, wondering how he could prepare him for the final crushing revelation.

'What do you mean?' he asked carefully.

'They were together?'

'Yes.'

'In my wife's room?'

'Yes.'

'In bed together?'

'It seems so. Yes.'

'Christ Jesus, damn the whoring pair of them!' Frank cried and turned away, covering his face with the blankets.

Richard read of the fire in the newspaper on his way back from the county hospital. It was the kind of tragedy that so often called for sympathy – a momentary sympathy and thrill of horror, mixed with shamefaced satisfaction that it had happened to someone else – before one passed on to less disturbing news. But it was different when someone you knew was involved. It couldn't be dismissed so easily. He had become friendly with Frank since he had moved into Commander Barnwell's room. He had helped him with his exercise. They had talked.

'Dreadful, isn't it?' said Keelan Lambert, who was accompanying him.

He tried to imagine what it would be like to get such news. Husbands and wives were bound by deep ties – like two branches grafted together. He remembered little things – childhood images trapped in memory: his father's hand laid momentarily on his mother's as they sat at table; laughter from their bedroom at night; his mother straightening his father's tie and drawing her finger in a delicate gesture along his cheek.

'The poor man was just beginning to pull round after his operation,' Keelan said.

Richard touched his finger reflexively to a light dressing on the left side of his neck where it met the collarbone. The wound was beginning to smart a little.

'Giving you trouble, is it?' Keelan asked.

'Stings slightly. That's all.'

To supplement the work of the new drugs, Doctor Staples had decided that the phrenic nerve in his neck should be temporarily crushed. This would relax the diaphragm and push up his lung. The introduction of air into the peritoneal cavity would push the lung up even further and give the diseased part a chance to rest.

'The operation didn't take long, anyway,' Keelan comforted.

'You could hardly call it an operation – ten minutes on the table and a local anaesthetic,' Richard replied.

He laid aside his paper and allowed himself to be lulled into a rhythmical vacuity by the swaying of the ambulance. Through the glass in front, he watched the greying head of Marty with the topped end of a cigarette behind his left ear. Keelan was a soothing presence beside him. Their bodies touched gently and came apart as they rounded a bend. Their steadying hands met along the seat. She let her fingers linger on his and smiled.

'Don't look now,' she squeezed his hand, 'but old spoilsport is watching in the mirror.'

They laughed in shared amusement. He felt suddenly happy at being alive. It was something he had not felt for a very long time.

Frank's door was closed when he got back and there was a notice on it saying that he was not to be disturbed. He was under sedation, Sister Cooney informed him, and was best left alone until he had absorbed the shock.

The following morning Richard was taken down to the treatment room and given his first induction of air. The experience was enough to keep him preoccupied for some time. He spent most of that day wrestling with discomfort and nausea. Whenever he sat up, the pressure on his chest was intense. His stomach seemed to be floating on a rising tide that compressed it against his sternum. At the back of his mind was the fear that he had been given too much air, that his lungs could not sustain the pressure, that they would collapse as Commander Barnwell's had collapsed.

The notice was off Frank's door by the time he was able to move about again and the door itself was open. It was late afternoon, with the darkness already lurking in the corners, when he went in. Frank was lying back on the pillows with his eyes closed. Richard was about to slip out again, when he stirred and opened them.

'I hope … I haven't disturbed you,' Richard said awkwardly.

'No,' Frank said in a tired voice, 'not at all.'

'I … read about it in the papers,' Richard said, not knowing how to begin. 'I'm very sorry.'

Frank grasped his proffered hand and said nothing.

'It must … have been … a dreadful shock.'

'God help us all!' Frank said and turned his head away. He roused himself with an effort, sniffed and shook his head vigorously. 'Sit for a little, like a good fellow.'

Richard sat on the side of the bed and looked at the floor. 'It's a strange world, isn't it?' he said.

'Youth is the best time,' Frank said quietly after a while. 'There's still hope then.'

'Yes.'

The room was full of darkness now, except for a bright triangle near the door where the light from the corridor fell.

'I was twenty-three that summer,' Frank whispered. 'There'll never again be a summer like it. Never!'

Richard sat helplessly and listened to him cry. There was nothing he could say, nothing he could do.

Like the sun peering from behind a cloud, Arty began to brighten and beam again. The notice came down from his door. One day it was there and the next it was gone. Neither Sister Cooney nor the doctors made any comment, but its disappearance was noted.

Ted Nugent, as might be expected, showed no such delicacy.'How's the typhoid or whatever-it-was, then?' he asked.

'I could have been a little hasty in my diagnosis,' Arty allowed with an embarrassed smile.'I'm no doctor, you know.'

'You can say that again!' Ted laughed.

'Hey!' Arty said, anxious to change the conversation.'Do you remember Vincent Finn?'

'Sure. What about him?'

'I had a letter from him. He's in a sanatorium in England.'

'What could he expect – running off like that!' Ted was indifferent to Vincent's fate.'The fellow was out of his … ' He stopped carefully, remembering Arty's condition.'He had no sense.'

'He may be coming back, you know,' Arty said, ignoring or not noticing Ted's remark. There was something about the prospective return of Vincent that cheered him.'He says the doctor over there is trying to arrange it.'

'Coming back here? He must be off his … he must be joking!' Ted said.

The letter from Lily came on the morning of the funeral. It lay around the office for a day or two, until someone had time to open it and send it back with a brief note, giving the time and circumstances of Elsie's death.

The letter itself had been short, its tone bleak. Lily was on the point of having what might yet prove to be only the first stage of a thoracoplasty. There were complications that she didn't understand – something to do with the fluid they kept draining off, something arising out of the chronic empyema. The doctors were so evasive that it was impossible to get anything definite from them. She now suspected that they had known long before and were breaking it to her gradually.

She was very depressed and pessimistic about the future. Vincent was getting treatment again. She spent most of her time in tears. She was sick with worry about everything.

It's like being caught in a huge sticky web – the more you struggle, the more entangled you get. Did you ever feel that it would be nice to give up struggling and close your eyes and sleep and never wake any more?

21

She lay propped up in pain and wondered when it was she had begun to loathe her body – she who had always been so proud of her figure and liked to pirouette in front of the glass after stepping from her clothes, admiring the slim smoothness of her thighs, the trim concavity of her belly, the neatness of her breasts, her skin with the sculptured texture of marble, her neck slender as the stem of a wineglass, and the bound-up hair in which fire lurked and leaped.

Pain was a living organism grafted into her. It gnawed at her like a ravenous animal. It burned and raged through her like a fever, until she began to imagine that she was no longer herself, no longer human at all, but the heart of fire, the savage tooth, the embodiment of the very essence of pain.

What was she now but a maimed thing, repugnant and ugly, which no love could ever be large enough to embrace? There could never now be that bridal night she had dreamed of, that uninhibited leap into love and happiness. Vincent had sworn that he would love her to the grave and beyond. What would he say, what would he think, what would he feel, if he saw her now?

It was as if the operation had excised her will to live. She lay, apathetic, dull as the lustreless droop of her hair on the pillows. She had been taken back to Ardeevan and put in one of the observation wards. But for her there was no sense of homecoming. Mrs Doran was gone, Elsie was dead. If Elsie could be taken so easily, what hope was there for anyone? What was the use in struggling? Better to surrender quietly to that hell of pain, to slide in to it, to crumble and fold like burning straw, to merge and coalesce and become one with it, until, phoenix-like, she floated away on the other side, whole and free.

When her mother came and sat beside her, twisting her fingers nervously and pulling on and off her gloves, lifting and laying down her basket in agitation, Lily rallied a little. Her father, a neat, spare man, sat on the bed and stroked her hand and said very little beyond the commonplace, putting all his affection and concern into that quiet gesture. He scrutinised her face anxiously as she listened to her mother, and when her eyes turned languidly towards him, he smiled and stroked her hand more earnestly. But when she turned back to her mother again, his face resumed its worried, searching frown of concentration, his ear attuned below the level of conversation to the pain and weariness in her voice.

Once, moved beyond composure by something he heard or saw, he rose abruptly and stood with his back to them, facing out over the sodden countryside. Behind him his wife's voice went on, chiding gently about the fruit that had remained untouched on her locker, the meals returned uneaten.

'You'll have to try and eat, dear, to make yourself strong again. If I peel an orange now, will you eat a little – just to please your father? He took the day off from work specially to come with me. He's worried about your not eating.'

When they had gone, Lily cried for them in their helplessness, feeling, for all her weakness, stronger than them, realising that it was easier to contemplate one's own death than the death of someone loved. Something in their need of her pulled her back from the seductive slide into oblivion. She would have to exert her will and fight against the pain-consuming darkness, if not for her own sake, then for theirs.

Old Barnwell is dead. Mike Quinn is dead. Elsie Hogan is dead. Every week, somebody dead. It's enough to drive anybody off his rocker. Talking of which, you'll laugh when you hear I went a bit bonkers myself for a while. I don't know what came over me. The Strange and Singular Lunacy of A. Byrne, you could call it! Anyway, I'm OK again. I got this notion that I'd some terrible disease – as if the Con wasn't terrible enough – and everybody would catch it off me. The worst thing about it was that nobody would believe me until it was too late. The old fellow even came to see me, so you know how bad I was. Seeing him, of course, didn't make me any better. He just sat there, scratching his head with those black fingernails and telling my mother there was never anything like that on his side of the family. It was all her fault, if you could believe him. Maybe it was, too, because anyone would want to be a little round the bend to marry him ...

It was easy now to write to Vincent about his father's visit in a flippant, amusing way, but it hadn't been like that at all.

'You'll disgrace us all,' Arty's father had said. 'What will people say? It's bad enough to have a son of mine in this place. But getting treatment in the mad house!'

'Wasn't I born and reared in a mad house?' Arty had retorted harshly.

'What do you mean, boy? What do you mean?'

'He means nothing at all,' his mother had intervened, 'except that you've upset him. Will you leave the poor fellow alone? The doctor said he wasn't to be excited.'

Then his father was off on another tack. 'It's them doctors is all to blame. I want a word with them fellows. I want to know what they meant by sending a son of mine to –'

'I'm no son of yours,' Arty interrupted.

'Are you out of your …?' his father stopped and looked in a startled manner at his mother, who had given him a sharp dig, then began to cough.

'I think you're looking much better today, Arty.' His mother had stepped in to fill the embarrassed silence. 'Have you put on some weight?'

Did I tell you Madeleine came to see me again shortly after you left? She's better to talk to than to write to, if you know what I mean. I hardly ever write letters any more. I got fed up of all that daft nonsense. You were right about pretending. She loves music and says she'd like to sing in a band. If I was outside, she said she could telephone me every day for nothing, if I gave her the number of a phone box and arranged to be there at a certain time …

Madeleine's second visit had been before his long slide into melancholy. During the succeeding weeks he had not written – except to send her an enigmatic note warning her to keep away. Her response had been a spate of anxious letters which he had let accumulate in his locker. When the cloud lifted, he had taken them out and read them. Moved by her obvious concern, he had written to explain that he had been through a bad time, but was better now.

Madeleine replied with the news that she had been promoted and was moving to a town not twenty miles away. 'I'd be able to come and see you oftener – if you'd like me to, Arty.'

He pondered the implications of this for a few days, uncertain whether to welcome it or feel alarmed. It would mean telling her everything – and telling the full truth about himself had never been easy. It would also mean giving the signal for the relationship to develop. Did he really want it to continue? Something in

187

the loneliness and fear he had experienced during his ordeal told him that he did.

> She knows all about me being bonkers and everything and doesn't seem to mind. She's coming to see me again soon.

Meanwhile his health was improving. As soon as the visits to the mental hospital had ended, he had been put on streptomycin and PAS, like several of the younger patients. The reputation of the new drugs had preceded them and a ripple of optimism ran through the sanatorium, though Doctor Staples had been careful to stress that they were still in the experimental stage. But it would have taken a lot more than the doctor's understandable caution to dispel the general euphoria.

Richard was having a lean time. He was in a state of perpetual nausea. The ringing in his ears persisted. He was sore from constant injections. He could neither lie nor sit comfortably, and when he walked about, the pressure under his collarbone was intense.

Still, there was reason for optimism. He had put on weight. The sputum had decreased and for two successive tests had been negative. Three negative reports in a row would be a strong indication that the disease had been arrested. All that remained after that was to continue the treatment until the lesions calcified. So for him the next test – whose result he was awaiting – would be crucial.

Meanwhile there was Keelan Lambert with whom he was developing some kind of tentative relationship. She was stationed now on the male floor and visited him frequently – sometimes in the line of duty, sometimes for a few minutes when her work was finished, often – as now, when she should have been elsewhere – for an illicit cigarette.

'Congratulations!' she said, as she blew smoke carefully through the open window. 'I saw it on your chart.'

'Saw what?' Richard had laid aside his book to watch her, standing there with that bright, scrubbed freshness young nurses always seem to have.

'Your third test. It's negative.'

He smiled back at her, shaking his head, pleased but wary, in case it might be premature. 'Are you sure?'

'Of course I'm sure. I told you I saw it on your chart. You don't seem very excited.'

'I am excited,' he laughed, 'way down somewhere.'

'That's the funny thing about you,' Keelan said. 'There's such a lot of you way down somewhere. You take life very seriously.'

'Wouldn't you, if you were in my position?'

'I suppose so. Anyway, it's good news, isn't it?'

'Great!'

'You'll be out before you know where you are.'

'Will I?'

'There you go again,' she chided, 'looking for trouble around every corner.'

'There you go again,' he laughed. 'It's always summer and you're walking through fields of daisies.'

Since Christmas his feelings about Keelan were ambivalent. He was flattered by her interest. In the desert in which he found himself, her youth and beauty shone like some exotic bloom. At times he felt tender and protective towards her, but sometimes he surprised himself by the hatred he felt for her, because she was healthy and free and had no need of him. For her the world was full of young men whose bodies were untainted by disease and these – he persuaded himself – were the ones she really craved, having no care for him at all, except some morbid interest

189

in a diseased thing, which, presently, she would thrust aside with a disdainful shudder.

Sometimes, when he thought he might die, as Eileen had died, some deep and insatiable curiosity about life and living in him, some craving to take with him a deeper knowledge of women and their essence made him long to lie in love with her, to taste the sweetness of her mystery, to see the world just once from a vantage point where the lost and lonely flesh that is man and woman comes together in a healing synthesis.

An inquest had been held and a verdict of accidental death returned. It was reported in all the newspapers. But nowhere was there a mention of the exact circumstances in which they had been found. Frank was grateful for that, at least. Votes of sympathy were passed and the matter forgotten.

For a long time he was obsessed by the image of them in bed together. It floated mockingly through his sleep and came like a mirage between his eyes and the daylight. He saw them laughing carelessly together, ruttish and brutal in their casual coupling. He saw their tangled limbs relax and slide into sleep, arms trailing. He saw the spilled spirits and the creeping flames.

What had been her last thoughts? Triumph after conquest? Warm animal feeling of satiety? Relief at the momentary quieting of a tyrannical appetite? Disgust and self-loathing? She would never find now whatever it was she had been looking for from life. Neither would he, because all he had ever wanted was her love. He prayed that she would be forgiven for being herself and following her nature. He had tried to forgive her; there was nothing else he could do.

He prayed he might be forgiven whatever deficiency in him

190

had contributed to her waywardness. All his life he had sought her pardon for the failure which she either could not or would not spell out for him. He raked through their life together, looking for clues. But nothing presented itself. Was it some insensitivity in his nature that had failed to respond to the nuances of the relationship, some obtuseness of perception that had prevented him from seeing, as it still prevented him from understanding?

In an effort to distract him, Sister Cooney had encouraged Doctor Staples to draw up a new and exacting regimen of exercises for him which she would supervise herself. She had him out of bed, touching his toes, bending and swaying with outstretched arms, leaning this way and that, rotating his hips, raising and lowering his shoulders, until his mind was numbed and he obeyed her commands like a robot.

Much of the exercise was done in front of a mirror so that he could see for himself and correct the sag on the right side where his ribs had been removed. There was always the danger of curvature of the spine. To correct the curve it was necessary to stretch the concavity and contract the convexity – in furtherance of which he spent a good deal of his time moving across the floor in a peculiar creeping posture, which Doctor Staples referred to as 'Klapp's crawl'.

He threw himself into the exercises with a kind of despairing frenzy. If he kept himself occupied, there was less time to think. Sister Cooney urged him to it. She was in each morning like a circus trainer to put him through his routine. She cracked her whip and he responded. There was something brutal and, at the same time, patient and caring about her single-mindedness. There was method in her toughness which he recognised and appreciated. She was pushing his body to the limits of its endurance to divert and ease the strain on his spirit. When the exercises finished for the day, he relaxed into numbness, his mind free and floating on a gently rocking tide.

More and more, as the days passed, he returned to that early summer, sealing his mind against what followed. There was a kind of peace in forgetfulness. But all the time, he was aware of the shutter in his memory; behind it, monsters prowled.

22

They were in the office, reviewing charts and assessing progress.

'Richard Cogley seems to be coming along nicely.' Doctor Staples lifted his eyes from the chart. 'We'll send him for another x-ray when he's completed his course of strep.'

'He's made a remarkable recovery,' Sister Cooney said.

'Yes. Maybe we'll be able to count him as one of our successes yet.'

'She opened another chart and handed it to him. 'What do you think of Frank O'Shea?'

Doctor Staples held the x-ray up to the light. 'He's quite a lot of muscle to build up there yet.'

'He's very determined – makes a great effort with the exercises.'

'Good!'

'Tragic – about his wife – wasn't it?'

'Worse even than it appeared,' Doctor Staples said knowingly. 'She was a lively piece, from what I hear – flying her kite all over the place. I believe she and the barman …' He raised his eyebrows and stopped.

'I was wondering about that,' Sister Cooney said thoughtfully. 'But how can anyone be sure?'

'I have it from the coroner himself. They were found in … ah … compromising circumstances.'

'Poor man!' Sister Cooney said. 'Does he know?'

'Unfortunately – yes. He had to be told.' He lifted his hands in a helpless gesture, then, letting them drop, he picked up the next chart. 'Did we – by the way – get some communication about that chap, Finn?'

'There is a letter somewhere,' Sister Cooney searched until she found it and handed it to him. 'They want to know when we'd have a bed. It seems he's fit to travel.'

'I'm in two minds whether we should have him at all. Fellows like him unsettle other patients. How do we know he won't discharge himself again after a week?'

'It wasn't the usual kind of thing.' Sister Cooney had sympathy for Vincent, who, until his departure, had been a model patient. 'You remember the incident of the girl and Doctor O'Connor-Crowley?'

'Oh, yes, that …' Doctor Staples said vaguely.

'There's a bed vacant in Ward 4.'

'I have somebody for that – chap of seventeen. Finn will have to wait his turn. Interesting case this one. Working in a flour mill. Lung coated with the stuff. It's essential to get him in straightaway. Boy called James Reville. I want him in this evening. You'll have to shuffle people around and give him a room to himself – isolate him. It's not TB, you see, but just as deadly for all that.'

February was wet, with gales that howled up the valley and rattled the glass doors leading to the verandah. The floor-covering near the doors was dulled with damp, like the bloom on a plum. Because the rain blew in gusts, the doors were usually closed and the glass clouded and wept, and the

194

world closed in and nothing existed at all except a diseased crew, buffeted and windswept, butting their way through the void.

Yet there was a sealed-in cosiness when darkness fell early and the lights came on. The wind fretted and slapped, like the brush of an animal body against the glass. It beat at the stonework and screamed about projections. It hammered glass and roof with vicious bursts of hail. The glass itself was converted into smudged mirrors which enlarged their ambience and distanced them from the storm.

It was the kind of weather Jack Carbery loved, when he could lie for hours, securely wrapped, and sleep – to wake again with the comfortable feeling that a warm meal was near and, after it, a pipe or cigarette and casual conversation with his friends. There was nothing he had to do to earn it, or nothing to threaten his security, except a too-rapid recovery, which he daily prayed against and which a good God would surely not allow – at least until summer came in and clothed a scarred earth with kindliness. His chronic disease, which erupted periodically like a benign volcano, was his insurance policy. He saw the new drugs as a threat to his well-being, and lived in dread of the day when they might be prescribed for him.

It was pleasant to lie and think of other Februaries and see himself abroad at dusk in the fields under a chilling rain, standing in a cart hunched up against the storm, bending and rising and bending again to toss turnips to the streaming cattle, listening to their soft thud in the mud and the straining of the horse as his hooves sucked and sank, the cattle lowing plaintively and the sharp crunch of their scooping teeth. Then back to the farmyard to untackle and fodder the horse, to strip off his own thatch of soaked sacking, and milk cows by the light of a lantern that swung from a hook in the roof and smelled sharply

195

in contrast with the milky smell of steaming cows and the less agreeable smell of fresh dung.

Supper at the kitchen table – bread coarsely cut and buttered, with none of the little refinements that were considered necessary for the family, who ate in another room. His clothes steaming as he bent to light a cigarette from a blazing splinter on the open hearth. Then out to his bed in a loft over the cowshed, leaving the family to draw in together in a cosy, alien-excluding unit around the flaming and hissing timber, to lie and smoke by the light of a candle and think of better days in the orphanage and wonder in unembittered fashion – for he had been happy there – about the mother who had abandoned him and the even shadowier lover who must have abandoned her.

No one was likely to recommend that a hopeless old chronic like him should be put on the new drugs at this stage, because they were still in short supply and there were many more interesting patients on whom to experiment. But Jack didn't know that and, even if he had known, it would only have given him a false feeling of security, because the threat from strepto-mycin, when it came, was not of a kind that he could have imagined or foreseen.

The first week of February had barely passed when Doctor Staples fired a warning shot across his bows. 'Beds! Beds! Beds!' He bustled in one day, rubbing his hands, a fashion of his when he had something unpleasant on his mind. 'What am I going to do for beds? Do you know how many people I have waiting for that bed or yours, Jack?'

Carbery looked at him warily, his eyes pleading not to be involved in such dangerous speculation, and shook his head slowly without speaking.

'Half a dozen, at least. Isn't that right, Sister?'

Sister Cooney looked sympathetically at Jack, but was constrained to nod in agreement.

'I could empty out this whole ward and fill it before evening with four new patients – four I could help, Jack; four that need help and need it now.'

Jack looked at the blankets and said nothing.

'It's the new Health Act – with free hospitalisation for infectious diseases,' the doctor explained to Sister Cooney. 'It's the new treatment as well. GPs have cottoned on to it and are clamouring for beds. They're building new sanatoriums – Ardkeen, Sarsfield's Court, Merlin Park – but until they're open, the pressure is on.'

He flicked through Jack's chart and snapped it shut abruptly. 'Put him down for x-ray, Sister, and we'll see.'

When they were back in the office again, Sister Cooney drew the matter down.

'That poor man has nowhere to go,' she said. 'He's no family. The people he's staying with don't want him.'

'We're running a sanatorium, not a retirement home,' Doctor Staples said harshly. 'Malingering is a luxury we can no longer afford to subsidise.'

'We can't throw him out in this kind of weather.'

'No, I suppose not,' Doctor Staples sighed. 'Maybe we could fix him up in the county home,' he said thoughtfully after some reflection. 'Get on to them, Sister, will you?'

Sometimes after the exercises, Sister Cooney stood and talked, while Frank lay back in bed, his breathing like the wind through dry leaves, and a rusty flush on his cheekbones. Frank was an easy man to talk to. He listened – at first with a curious air of detachment, as if he was an observer from another civilisation, or someone whose own experience had come to an end, someone who was waiting to embark on a journey and looked at the world with vacant eyes, his mind already in transit.

Hers was a friendly and comfortable presence and he was grateful to her for it. He was surprised at himself, at first, for feeling grateful, for being able to feel anything at all. He was surprised at himself for looking forward to her arrival and the hard, punishing exercises; for feeling anxious, if her coming was delayed; for hoping she would linger a minute afterwards and talk about the weather or some unusual flurry on the corridor.

The first time she brought him flowers – a posy of crocuses in a glass jar – he suddenly and unaccountably wept. She excused herself hurriedly and left, returning with a great bustle to announce her coming, when she had given him time to compose himself. He was sitting up, holding the jar in his cupped hands, admiring the delicate curve of the petals.

'It's a long time since anyone brought me flowers,' he smiled apologetically.

'They're nice, aren't they?' Sister Cooney said. Then, without a pause, but with a sharp change of tone and inflexion, she was the starched, crisp, efficient Sister. 'Now, if you'll hop out of bed and slip on your dressing gown, we'll start.'

Vincent had written to tell her that he was coming back. He wondered how she was and why she wasn't writing. He was worried about her silence. It wasn't like her. He would be coming over by boat and a male nurse would come with him as far as Dún Laoghaire. He could travel well enough on his own, if only they'd let him. But that was the way they did things over there – well-meaning but fussy.

She would have to drag herself out of her lethargy and write. Some patients got others to write for them when they were low, but there was nothing Lily wanted to say to Vincent that she could ask anyone to write. She seemed to lack all will or decision. In the early days after the operation, when she was tightly bound in a many-tailed bandage to which weights were sometimes attached, and with drainage tubes still trailing from her, she had managed to scribble notes to him almost every other day. Now, more lightly bound and sitting more comfortably in what the doctors called 'Fowler's position', she found many reasons for indecision and delay.

The irreversibility of her mutilation lay like a fallen tree across her spirit. She no longer combed and preened herself. When the nurses – who, to encourage morale, insisted that every patient, however ill, should wash – came to help her, she submitted with an indifference that alarmed them. She suffered meekly the humiliations of the bedpan. Something in her that had, at first, revolted in anger and frustration at her own helplessness, now shrivelled and atrophied. She would lie for hours – days even, for she had lost all interest in time – in an abstraction of pain, her bruised mind slipping and struggling and relapsing into a slough. The future, which once had seemed to her a long, grassy vista into distant sunlight, was now a black impenetrable vapour, blowing towards her menacingly, like some poisonous gas, and threatening to envelop her.

She would have to write to Vincent. His name broke into syllables, fragmented further into letters, and whirled, like flecks of butter in a churn, round and round in her mind. Round and round, intermittently, through the days it spun, crystallising now and again – before breaking apart once more – into the essence of him, an image, like sudden flashes on a screen, of his diffident smile when they first met, the touch of his hand on her elbow as he guided her to a seat down that summer lane.

What could she say to him except that she felt her life – their life together – slipping away; that whether she survived or slid wearily from her broken body, there was no longer any prospect of happiness for them; that he should forget her and make his own world without her?

The letter, when she came to write it – painfully, word by word over many days – was quite different to what she had intended.

I love you and that's all I know – all that's worth knowing. If only we realised in time, we wouldn't waste our lives on trash. Why is the best thing in the world tied to the least lasting? If only I could see you – just once? All our dreams, Vincent, where are they? Our end is like our beginning – we know nothing.

She read it over many times, letting her tears fall unchecked on the page. She hoped Vincent would understand, would draw consolation from the knowledge that her life had not been empty, because her love would live on, warming with its humanity a cold and, possibly, hostile universe.

23

Arty was sitting up in bed, his hair shining from a liberal application of something that looked and smelled like perfumed vaseline and came from a jar labelled Easi-Gro. Over his pyjamas he had put on a new Fair Isle pullover which had been his mother's Christmas present. He was busily pruning his nails with a pair of scissors and trying to make up his mind about the proper degree of flippancy to adopt for his conversation with Madeleine, when the romance of his afternoon was suddenly eclipsed by the strident voice of his father, grating like a rusty wheel on a dry axle.

'I was looking for you all over. Since when did they move you down here?'

'What are you doing here? Is it the end of the world or what?' Arty looked at him without welcome. 'I was expecting a visitor.'

'A lady, God help us, by the dolled-up look of you. Isn't your father visitor enough for you?' He wiped his drooping moustache with the back of his hand.

Arty had a whiff of his alcoholic breath as he leaned forward to sit. 'Are you on a booze-up or what?' he asked belligerently.

'That's what I get for coming to see you and your mother in bed with the flu,' his father protested indignantly.

'Is she all right?' There was concern in Arty's voice – a concern that seemed to annoy his father.

'I was ten times worse myself and got over it on my feet,' he said in casual dismissal, opening his raincoat and reaching inside for a cigarette. 'You don't smoke, I suppose.' He waved the box vaguely in Arty's direction, extracted a cigarette, lit it and immediately started to cough.

'You'll kill yourself with those things,' Arty said in a tone in which hope was mingled with disgust.

'Devil a much you – or anybody else – would care!'

Arty acknowledged by his silence the truth of the remark.

'Why did they shift you down here?' His father leaned back and blew smoke towards the ceiling.

Arty looked round at Jack Carbery and the five others who had been moved to the ground floor with him. 'Shortage of beds,' he said. 'This used to be a recreation room. People are dying to get in here now. Did you know that?'

'God, you're a gas turn!' His father's laugh changed quickly into a prolonged cough.

'Dying to get out of here too,' Arty said.

'Don't push your luck,' his father advised, rubbing his eyes with his finger. 'Tell us,' he continued, 'a butty of mine came in here last week, Sandy Cooper – you know Sandy from Chapel Lane? Where would I find him?'

'Upstairs,' Arty said, feeling suddenly cheered. 'Maybe you'd better go up and see him – now.'

'No hurry,' his father said. 'He won't be going any place, will he?'

'Listen,' Arty pleaded in desperation, 'will you do me a favour and feck off up to see him. I told you I was expecting someone. Sandy'll be delighted to see you.'

'That'll be a change from my son, won't it?' his father chided. 'Sure, I'll go up to Sandy, but first I want to see this great one you're expecting.' He raised one end of his moustache in a sardonic grin.

'It's nobody you'd know,' Arty sniffed shortly.

'Nobody I'd know!' his father mimicked. 'Is she a black woman or what – you're so ashamed of her?'

They both looked up together as the door opened and Madeleine came hesitantly forward.

'This is her!' Arty hissed. 'Now, will you go?'

'God, you're doing all right for yourself,' his father's rasping voice filled the ward.

Madeleine stood to look around, then, seeing Arty, smiled and walked towards them.

'Where'd you pick her up?' his father whispered as he stood and raised his hat in a gesture that was too elaborate.

'Sshhh!' Arty said, a cloud on one side of his face, while the other turned with a smile to greet Madeleine.

'Hello!' he said.

'Hello, Miss!' His father nodded agreeably and settled his hat back on his head.

'Goodbye!' the dark side of Arty hissed. 'You'll find your man upstairs.'

His father brushed the chair he had been sitting on and, with a flourish, invited Madeleine to sit down. He showed no inclination to leave.

'How are you, Arty?' Madeleine smiled, then looked in an enquiring way towards his father.

'This is … my father. He's just going,' Arty said ungraciously. He was twisting his fingers and not at all at ease.

'Pleased to meet you, Miss.' His father extended his oil-blackened hand for her to shake.

203

'Pleased to meet you, Mr Byrne. My name's Madeleine.' She shook his hand firmly and sat down.

There was a pause as they looked at one another and adjusted their minds to the needs of conversation. Arty's father was the first to speak.

'What line of business would you be in? I'm in bicycles myself.'

'He's a first cousin to Sir Walter Raleigh,' Arty ventured and laughed nervously.

'He's a real comedian, this fellow,' his father appealed to Madeleine, 'isn't he?'

Madeleine laughed and looked in amusement at Arty.

'Would you be in the bank or that?' his father probed.

'I'm a telephonist,' Madeleine said.

'Give us a ring sometime!' Arty was getting more and more desperate.

'On the wireless he should be,' his father said. '*Much Binding in the Marsh* or something like that.'

'Don't forget your man upstairs,' Arty pleaded.

'Terrible weather, isn't it?' Madeleine said conversationally.

'Did you come far?' Arty's father asked.

'Your man is in Ward 4,' Arty prompted. 'He was enquiring about you.'

'Tryin' to get rid of me.' His father looked at Madeleine archly. 'You'd better mind yourself with this fellow. Doesn't want his old man around doing gooseberry.'

'I don't know which of you is the greatest joker,' Madeleine laughed.

Arty's father stood up and patted his hat lower on his forehead. 'Two's company,' he said. 'A man knows when he's not wanted.'

'Any sensible man would,' Arty said sourly.

His father opened the lid of Arty's sputum mug and dropped the butt of his cigarette inside. 'I'll see you on the way back.'

'No need to hurry,' Arty told him. He leaned over to catch his father's sleeve and hissed, 'No feckin' need to come back at all!'

His father ignored him and smiled graciously at Madeleine. 'On the telephone, eh? I could never get the hang of them things at all.'

'You get used to it,' Madeleine said.

'We'll be seein' you, then.'

'Not if we can see you first!' Arty spat.

At the door his father turned to wink familiarly at Madeleine. 'Mind what I said, now, girlie,' he grated in a raucous roar that turned all heads. 'Your man there is a quare hawk, I'm tellin' you. Look at him – throwin' his eye up your skirt – and it no time at all since he gave up wettin' the bed!'

Most of the hour Richard spent pacing up and down the corridor, stopping at windows to look out between the buildings at bare trees and transparent hedges. By the end of February he was on a second hours' exercise, and Sister Cooney, who had watched his restless pacing and had seen that he was bored, found him some light work to do.

'That library is in a right mess since Jim Kielthy took it over,' she said. 'You're a fellow who's fond of books. How would you like to arrange and classify and catalogue the lot?'

'I'd love to,' he said.

'Good! I'll fix it for you with Matron.'

The following day she was back with a hard-covered, exercise book and a pot of glue. 'Everything's arranged. Your first hour – or as much of it as you care to spend there. The book is for the catalogue. The glue is for pasting the various classifications on to the shelves. Kielthy won't trouble you, by the way.

We've … ah … ,' she smiled, 'retired him on pension. Jack Carbery will take on the distribution of books. Jack's a good careful fellow. You can explain to him about your system and he'll put the books back where he found them.'

'Right!' he said. 'When do I start?'

'Now if you like.' Her smile broadened. 'I'll have Nurse Lambert take you down in the lift. Matron says she may give you a hand today – or, indeed, at any time when things are slack on the wards.'

Richard blushed like a schoolboy.

'I'll send her down to you,' Sister Cooney laughed. At the door she could not resist a parting shot. 'I suppose you could classify her under "Romance".'

There was a skittishness about Sister Cooney lately, he noted. She was more than usually cheerful. He wondered if it was the promise of spring.

'Like all nurses, you're a martinet at heart,' Frank gasped. He stopped swinging his arms and stood with hands on hips, looking at her, his head and shoulders heaving. He sat down on the bed and let his arms sag. 'Thanks, Sister – for the push and all. I needed it.'

He felt grateful to her for dragging him out of the pit and back into the daylight. It was a drab light and there was no great cheer in it, but it was, at least, better than the dark. He joined his hands and sat looking down at them, watching his thumbs circle each other like wary combatants.

'There's something I'd like to tell you,' he began slowly, 'that is, if you wouldn't think it an intrusion.'

'You don't have to tell me anything.' Sister Cooney sensed that he was about to confide something that he might later regret. Patients – under the stress of emotion – sometimes did that.

'It wasn't much of a marriage, you know,' he said after a while.

'Are you sure you want to talk about it?'

'That made it worse, you see. There was nothing to hold on to. You have more to reproach yourself with. You feel more guilt. You think of all the things you might have done and didn't. You feel like a climber who unties the rope when he finds it irksome and, because of your carelessness, someone behind slips and falls to his death.'

'Frank,' Sister Cooney said quietly, 'I know all about your wife's death.'

He raised his hand to his mouth in a gesture of dismay and held it suspended there a few inches from his face. 'All?' he whispered.

'All.'

'About herself and ... O'Gorman ... too?'

'Yes. So you know and I know that you, of all people, have nothing to feel guilty about.'

Frank covered his face with his hands and sat rocking himself backwards and forwards, like a child seeking comfort in a healing rhythm. 'Who else knows?' he asked.

'Doctor Staples – no one else.'

He lowered his hands and looked at her. 'I'm glad you know. I wanted to tell you.' He gestured helplessly – an awkward, futile action without grace in it. 'You mustn't think badly of her, though,' he added.

'No – and you mustn't ever again think badly of yourself.'

'You see, I knew her.' Frank allowed his tears to flow unchecked. 'Nobody else did. Nobody else at all.'

There were fears that the chronic empyema, which the thoracoplasty had been expected to cure, would recur on the other side. Lily had experienced pain there and her temperature fluctuated

207

wildly. Doctor Staples had examined her carefully, then called for cannula and trocar and performed the aspiration that she had been assured would never again be necessary. He drew off some fluid and relieved the pressure, then went back to the office, where he shook his head gloomily as he pored over the report that had come back with her from Seapark. If the thing persisted, her only remaining lung would collapse under a bag of pus and she would die, because she could no longer breathe.

Lily lay in mild shock afterwards, while nurses fussed about her with hot-water bottles and held a cup of strongly sweetened tea for her to sip. Her mind was capable of thinking of nothing at all. She felt battered into numbness by the sustained assault on her diminishing reserves. She felt her spirit shrivel in her, withdrawing in alarm from the coldness of her extremities. Her eyes were closed against the glare of lights overhead, but still their dazzle came through. It occurred to her hazily that her own condition was like that of a bulb she had once seen when the power had been suddenly cut down and the light had dimmed to the faintest red glow in the filament.

24

The library was a comfortable brown room with tall windows to floor level and doors opening on to the terrace with its crumbling balustrade and ornamental urns. The books were housed in mahogany bookcases which covered the walls from floor to ceiling. In the centre of one wall there was a Palladian mantelpiece in grey marble and above it a shield, bearing the coat of arms of the Challoner family. The room had one long table with half a dozen chairs ranged around it. The carpet was a faded red. The floor at the edge was stained a dark oak. A few cane chairs with bright cushions stood near the windows, whose heavy drapes matched the carpeting.

To open the door and step inside was to leave the atmosphere of a hospital. This, and the musty smell of books, was its chief attraction for Richard. On the shelves, the books themselves were in a chaotic jumble, stacked in piles, or stuffed in, spine first. The disorder pleased him. There would be hours of satisfying work in sorting and rearranging.

'Did you ever see such a mess!' Keelan laughed. 'Where on earth are we going to start?'

'We'll clear one shelf onto the table here, and then we'll see.'

'We may as well start at the top, then.' She dragged over a

stepladder, climbed it, and began to hand him books. When the shelf was cleared, she stepped down and asked, 'Now, what?'

'We'll make a rough division into fiction and nonfiction for a start,' he said. 'We can subdivide later.'

They sorted through the books and divided them into two lots. Then they replaced the nonfiction temporarily, as the volumes came to hand, and started on the second half. The sight of her body, poised above him as she stretched and leaned, distracted him, and he stood to watch her, until she turned with a questioning half-smile to hand down another bundle.

'Perhaps you've had enough for today?' Keelan was suddenly gone and Nurse Lambert was in her place. 'You sit there. I'll put the nonfiction back with the rest. We can leave the fiction on the table until tomorrow.'

On the way up in the lift she was herself again and kissed him hurriedly between floors. But it was Nurse Lambert who stepped briskly out of the lift and escorted him to his door.

He was not sure which he wanted her to be and was still puzzling about it next day when she called to take him down. She was a pleasant girl, but he didn't really know her. He felt now that it was impossible to know other people until one saw how they reacted in extremity or under pressure. He had known very little about himself until he was face to face with death. Eileen's death had made the lot of them aware of depths in themselves and in each other that they had not known of before.

'Are you going back to university?' Keelan asked as they worked.

'You're talking about a world that seems light years from here. I can't even begin to think about it.' He walked over to the window and tapped on the glass. 'I'm a goldfish in a bowl,' he said. 'That may or may not be reality out there. I don't know any

210

more. The whole thing may be an illusion. Do you realise I haven't walked on grass for almost a year?'

'It's still the same grass.'

'But I'm not the same person. I don't mean just physically – that, too, of course. I'll never be the same again.'

'Why not?'

'Because so many things that seemed important aren't important any more.'

What was important now? People, friends, someone to love – and beyond that nothing at all.

Frank folded the brief letter from his solicitor and put it back into its envelope, before tossing it negligently aside.

'That's that!' he said with an expansive feeling of well-being. 'As of Friday last, I am without house or home – and I never felt better.'

Sister Cooney looked at him with a polite, questioning smile and waited for him to continue or change the subject, as he thought fit.

'I've sold out, lock, stock, and barrel – particularly barrel – because I hated that pub,' he explained. 'It's something I always wanted to do.'

'You've sold the lot?'

'The pub, the land, everything!'

'But where will you live?'

'Hotel, guesthouse, somewhere ...' he said vaguely. 'Anywhere – as long as it's not Moyalla. I'm tired of country villages where everybody lives in everybody else's pocket.'

'What about your job?'

'Time enough to worry about that. I could always retire on disablement pension, find some quiet town, a town on a river, where there'd be some fishing. I might buy a little business, maybe a newsagency – pipes, tobacco, a few books, stationery, fishing tackle. There'd be time to read, have a chat with people, walk in the sun, make a new life.'

… I could have belted him with a bicycle chain. What's the use in having ould fellows, when you don't need them any more? If they had any understanding or decency in them, they'd die and leave you in peace. Mothers are all right, I suppose, and you'd miss them fussing about the place, but ould fellows are like the hind tits of a cow – no good for use or ornament. All they ever do is booze and belch and kick up stink and take the best seat at the fire. There ought to be a law against them. Madeleine said she didn't mind, but you could see his lordship was going down like a dose of castor oil. Still, she didn't puke outright and that's something. But the afternoon was done for. She's a grand girl, though. She's coming again soon.

About Lily, all I know is that she's not well. She hasn't been for a long time. But don't worry. The news that you're coming soon will lift her out of it.

Mrs Moore sat with Lily's pale hand in hers and talked with desperate gaiety about the coming of spring. What she did not say – what she could not say – was that the cold high days with their lengthening light terrified her. Their brittle and unsettling promise had already crept into the dark corners of her house and laid bare its emptiness. Winter had been a huddle of darkness and hope, but now spring laid its probing finger on the hidden dust and called for recognition and ruthless change. Already it was whispering at the roots of grass, inciting it to rise, breathing on sheltered primroses, preaching its false gospel of resurrection and renewal, while underneath, the rot continued, the trampled snail returned to clay and beauty drew sustenance from a grave.

She looked at Lily's shrunk and sanded face, abstracted on

some pinnacle of pain, and saw it lanced by the fierce thrust of grass and sucked dry by the brutal assault of flowers. She clasped her daughter's hand in despair, as if she would pull her back from the falsely-beckoning light. The faint pulse of Lily's wrist under her fingers was a knife-twist in her heart. 'Don't give in, love!' she whispered fiercely. 'Don't give in!'

Lily's hand fluttered negatively in her own and a harrowed smile, fleeting as a wind's breath, stirred her lips and then they stretched back again into a tense, bloodless rictus.

Mrs Moore hadn't understood much of what Sister Duggan had told her about the recurrence of fluid and the aspiration that was again necessary. But she understood well enough that her daughter's life was slipping away. She sat on the bed, as on the sand of some ebbed sea, surrounded by a vast loneliness.

Early March with crows tumbling and swooping about the verandah after flung crusts, scraping the air in hoarse conflict.

Jack Carbery, fully dressed, sat on a chair beside his bed, looking up at them. The world, he thought, was a competitive place and the weakest went without. His cardboard suitcase lay ready, and he looked stiff and awkward in his shiny suit of blue serge and clumsily knotted tie. He watched as a homemaker, winging high, dropped its bundle of thin twigs and pushed itself into a steep dive to join the scramble.

At half-ten the ambulance would arrive to bring him to the county home. He took out of his waistcoat pocket a large watch which he had bought years before from a cheap-jack at a fair. It was a quarter past. The watch was reliable. It kept good time. He had paid ten shillings for it. It was the kind of thing a man might pass on to his son some day – if he had a son.

He noticed a ragged old crow fall away from the raucous

213

throng and glide to the ground. It stood about patiently until a crust dropped, then approached it with a sideways hopping motion and began to tear it. The old and the weak had to counter strength with cunning.

Jack stroked the watch affectionately with his finger and returned it to his pocket. Its strong beat had been a friend beside his ear at night as he lay thinking, or when he woke to have a quiet smoke in the darkness. With his few belongings it was home to him wherever he went. Its stopping would be like a death in the family.

Doctor Staples had got him a place in the county home. There was a little work to do, fetching and carrying about the kitchens, for which he would get ten shillings a week. It would be enough to keep his pipe pleasantly burning.

More crusts fell from the vicious scramble overhead. The old crow selected the largest one and dragged it to safety, out of the way of a pair of young birds chasing them down.

He would get to know the cook and ingratiate himself by being agreeable and doing her favours. It was the best way to make a snug billet for himself. There was nothing to be got from being disagreeable or testy. It would be important to be on the right side of the nuns too. A punctilious attention to prayers and strict religious observance would win their indulgence. There was a good living to be had for a shrewd man in an institution. He was blest to be free of the humiliations and the uncertainties of the farm.

Patients were flocking in for the new treatment. He no longer resented the loss of his bed. The future was more secure than he had ever dreamed possible. He would be back from time to time, but never again as a mendicant. His illness would stand to him in the other place too. With his history, no great physical demands could be made on him.

214

When the ambulance arrived, Sister Cooney came down to see him off.

'Well, Jack, how do you feel about your new home?'

'Fine, Sister, fine! God is good. He never closes one door but he opens another.'

He lifted his suitcase, which was light enough, and held out his hand. Sister Cooney took it and shook it warmly.

'They'll look after you well there,' she smiled. 'If they don't, let us know and we'll get on their track.'

She accompanied him out to the ambulance and closed the door behind him. As it slid down the avenue the old crow, which had risen and was circling warily, dropped down again to its crust. Sister Cooney stood and watched it in mild amusement, before turning and walking thoughtfully inside.

25

'Well, well, well!' Frank laughed. 'I never knew this Kielthy character was an atheist.'

'What makes you think he is?' Richard laid an armful of books on the table and strolled over to where Frank was sorting through a shelf.

Frank drew out a heavy copy of the Douay Bible and held it up. 'Who else would put this under fiction?'

He brought the Bible over to the table and sat down. It was pleasant to be among books again. He liked their feel and smell. It had been Sister Cooney's idea to take him down to help in the library. He was on an hour now and making good progress. Cogley was a nice quiet chap and they got on very well together.

'Have you seen his censored list?' Richard asked. 'I found them wrapped in a brown-paper parcel with "Dirty Books" scrawled on the outside with a purple pencil.'

'What kind of books did the learned Jim censor?' Frank smiled.

'Would you believe, *The Way of All Flesh*?'

'The title bothered him, I suppose,' Frank laughed.

Light splayed from his glasses as he looked up, glasses that brought into the room high-scudding clouds and an airy scrawl of branches.

'What was the thora like?' Richard asked suddenly, impelled by the curiosity that drives people to stare at and question the survivors of some calamity.

Frank rubbed his cheek thoughtfully with the heel of his fist before replying. 'Actually,' he said, 'it's like so many things in life – something you go through with once, because you have to. But you'd die rather than face it again.'

'Who's talking of dying on a fine day like this?'

They looked up to find Sister Cooney standing there. There was something youthful and springlike about her crisp, starched stance. She glanced at the book-laden table and at the general disarray. 'I'll have to send for Jim Kielthy to clear up this mess,' she laughed. 'I might have guessed that too many cooks ...'

'Actually, what you're looking at is creative disorder,' Frank protested lazily. 'We've been making great progress.'

'I can see that!' There was some nuance of intimacy in her tone that made Richard look up in surprise and then look at Frank. What he saw surprised him even more. It seemed to him that he had intercepted some secret communication between them.

Sister Cooney picked up a pile of books and began to replace them on the shelves. 'Enough for today,' she said. 'Any more progress like this and we'll be back where we started.' She turned to Richard, 'Oh, that reminds me,' she said. 'I've some good news for you. Doctor Staples says you may take a turn on the walks from now on. Half an hour will be enough to start with. You may take a stroll before you go up, if you wish. Frank and myself will put the rest of these back.'

Richard looked out at the sun and the trees with a quickening heart. For so long he had wondered if he would ever walk abroad again. Sister Cooney opened the French windows and he felt the air sweet on his face.

'Half an hour and no more,' she said. 'And when you come in, take the lift back up. You're in no condition yet to tackle the stairs.'

It was strange walking out after so long. It was like entering a new element. The free play of air around him defined and set the limits of his body in a way that he had completely forgotten. The exposure was a little frightening at first and instinctively he kept close to walls. Stepping off the concrete path onto gravel was a new sensation and he felt himself slide and stumble. The gravel came up, hard and irregular, through the soles of his slippers. Walking on it safely was a skill he would have to relearn. He stepped back onto the concrete and came round to the front of the building where the flowering cherries were just coming into bud on the lawn.

He stood and looked at them sway, feeling a unity with them as his body swayed to the same light breeze. A desire to touch them, to feel the smooth hardness of living wood again, brought him across the tarmacadam to the grass, which felt spongy and cool under him. There was a sensuousness about it that filled him with a desire to run shouting across it, to roll in it, to bury his face in it and sniff life out of its roots, to draw up his childhood from the green stems, to lie supine and shade his eyes from the sun and dream himself back into nature.

He had forgotten how things smelled. He pulled a fistful of grass and crushed it to his face. He sniffed at the warm bark of the cherries. He punctured the skin with his nail and tasted the sap. He chewed ribs of grass and swallowed green saliva. Out on the path again, he plucked and crushed a bay leaf and retired into the fragrance of his cupped hands. Wherever he walked, spring came at him with a rush, overwhelming him with sensation. He

218

felt like an infant staggering uncertainly out of doors for the first time into the infinitude of the universe.

At the decaying gate-lodge the ambulance stopped and Vincent got out. It was the last of several stops on the way down from Dún Laoghaire. His stomach still felt queasy and he was grateful for the fresh air. He leaned against the door of the ambulance and drew in the mossed and woody scent of trees. The call of rooks was loud in the pillared light, a call that was answered antiphonally, like receding echoes, from many quarters. The sun had brilliance but no heat. Somewhere near was the gurgle and trickle of water.

'All right if I walk up a bit?' he called to Marty, who was leaning forward with his elbow on the wheel and his open palm supporting his chin.

'As far as the last bend,' Marty said. 'You're not supposed to be out. You wouldn't want to get me into trouble, would you?'

'Just to the bend – to clear my head. It's the last I'll see of the outside for a long time.' He turned and walked slowly up the avenue. His legs were weak. There was no elasticity in them and nothing at all of the swelling sap, rising around him.

'How bad it would be,' Marty told himself callously as he watched him go, 'to have your bed and your bellyful and no worries at all!' He had been up since five to meet the boat from Holyhead and had an enormous appreciation of the manner in which he was being exploited.

Vincent stood and wiped cold sweat from his forehead. Twigs fell among the trees as the rooks rowed and ranted. He pulled a sticky brown bud from a drooping chestnut and peeled it naked. He held it to his nose and smelled its furry warmth, then spun it away from him with a twinge of regret at having torn it so wantonly. He was barely aware of the feeling. It was no more than a shadow on his deepening melancholy. Out of the same melancholy he grabbed irrationally at a whole branch, wrenched it off and tossed it among the trees. In some frustrated way he felt in himself a deep affront at the prodigality and profuseness of life around him.

The rooks in their frenzy of building were an affront too. There was nothing for him but a painful irony in their raucous clamour. They were slaves of their own chemistry, following a blind biological urge. What was in store for them and their young but the fox's maw, the poisoned grain and the angry scatter-shot of the farmer's gun?

Above him he heard the purr of engines, the slow, measured movement of cars in procession. Another funeral. He stood aside and leaned his back against the wire paling as the hearse came round the corner. Whose turn was it this time? He wondered if it was anyone he knew. Look, he wanted to shout at the tumbling rooks, here is the only certain reality. How efficient the place was – a model clearing house for death, turning out its yearly quota of corpses.

He blessed himself and dropped his eyes as the hearse passed. There was a wreath of laurel, intertwined with daffodils, on the coffin. People were walking after it – a young man about his own age with blank, staring face, a sobbing woman supported by her husband, and a girl, whose expression, as she passed, startled him. It was some young person in the coffin – son or daughter snatched prematurely.

The girl's expression, her appearance, the set of her head? He stepped out to have a better look. The sudden movement brought him into the path of a mourner, whose elbow struck him a glancing blow and sent him reeling. The man caught his arm and steadied him. 'Are you all right?'

'I thought I recognised somebody there,' Vincent said. 'Whose funeral is it?'

'A neighbour of mine,' the man said. 'Nice little girl she was too.'

Vincent felt his stomach heave with apprehension. 'What was her name?'

'Gold bless us and save us!' the man said. 'There's a power of young people after coming dead out of that place above.'

'Her name?' Vincent pleaded.

The man looked at him with a kindly face. He was short and middle aged and carried his cloth cap in his hand. 'A daughter of Paddy Moore of the Corn Market. That's who she was.'

'Lily!' Vincent cried.

'Yes, Lily,' the man said.

Vincent turned away and staggered to the wire and hung limp across it, his body trembling. He heard with awful clarity, above the shuffle of feet and the soft rolling of cars, the croak and caw of rooks and their tattered scuffling overhead.

Lily! The two of them holding hands in a summer lane. The scent of her hair in the darkness. Lily dead!

All our dreams, Vincent, where are they?

'She must not be dead,' he shouted mutely. 'If Lily is dead, there's nothing left at all.'

He pulled himself up and turned and ran down the avenue after her corpse, past slow-moving cars, whose occupants stared at him curiously. He brushed aside new-bursting buds that slapped at his face, until he stood by the rust-eaten iron gates, watching the hearse accelerate down the road. The cars passed out, one by one, and sped after it.

'Hey!' Marty called from the ambulance. 'Get in.'

Vincent walked out into the middle of the road and stood

there, his eyes fixed on the distant corner around which the hearse had disappeared. A car stopped beside him and a friendly voice called, 'Going to the funeral?'

Vincent stared at the man blankly.

'Are you coming or not?' The man was getting impatient. Behind him, cars were beginning to stop.

Vincent looked at him, as if seeing him for the first time.

'The funeral,' the man said again. 'Do you want a lift?'

He opened the door and waited. As if in a trance, Vincent got in and sat down beside him. The man let out the clutch and the car moved off.

26

The pale fire of spring daffodils warmed the room where Frank sat and read. Now and again he looked up from his book, stared at them intently and smiled. Even when he bent his head to the page, they came between him and the words. Their light, like the tail of a comet, spread spectacularly across his mind. After a while, he laid his book aside and sat there, his head tilted back, his thoughts adrift.

Soon he would be going out to start a new life. It was an unexpected bonus for a man of fifty-one. It would be foolish to expect too much after his experience, but there was an excitement in it, all the same. He had cut himself loose from the past and had good hopes of making a comfortable landfall. What was comfort only a roof over your head, a full belly, a fire, books to read and nothing on your mind? Health too, of course.

'You remember our last conversation here?' Doctor Staples smiled.

'That was several lifetimes ago,' Frank said, 'But I remember.'

He was seated again in Doctor Staples's office, watching the doctor examining his x-ray on an illuminated screen.

'I told you then your chances were good. I can now tell you that you have exceeded our expectations,' the doctor said.

'You consider it a success, then?'

'Certainly I do. You've done particularly well at the exercises.'

'It was one hell of a job, then,' Frank said, remembering the agony of the early days.

'Was, is and will be,' Doctor Staples reminded him. 'It's something you'll have to continue for the rest of your life. To ease off at any stage would undo all the good work.'

'I don't mind it now. I've got used to it. I rather like the whole penitential routine.'

'That's the spirit! Now, the next thing to talk about is when we can let you go.'

He had been there so long, had been so doubtful – and, until recently, so indifferent – about seeing the outside again that the mention of discharge took him by surprise. 'You mean I may go soon?'

'Yes, in a week or two. We'll have another x-ray, do some final tests and let you off. You'll have to report to the clinic regularly, of course – every week for a while and then once a month. If all goes well, you may be able to go back to school when the new year starts in the autumn. How do you feel about that?'

'I'll have to think about it,' Frank said vaguely.

He had practically made up his mind that he would never go back – certainly not to Moyalla and probably not to teaching. But there was no point in bothering Doctor Staples with the complexities of his private life.

'What I mean is you should have a reasonably clean bill of health by then,' Doctor Staples said.

He was tired of teaching, had already given too much of his life to it. He was tired of respectability, tired of the constant tug-of-war to pull the lively minds of children out of the fields and hedges, where wisdom and philosophy began, into the abstractions of formal learning. Too often he had seen education serve no better purpose than to impose limits of caution and doubt on vision and imagination. Far too often the village teacher was expected to be the creature of his employer, the school manager. His public utterances were examined for heresy, his private life combed for scandal. The good teacher was a safe man who spoke in mealy-mouthed platitudes, steeped himself in orthodoxy, made obeisance to all the right quarters, allowed his intellect and judgement to fossilise in the interests of ... what? His own security – a quiet, mindless life.

'Where will you go?' Sister Cooney asked.

'Into town for a bit. I'll get a room somewhere: hotel, guest-house. What do you think?'

'Guesthouse, maybe – less noise and you'd get more attention. What you need is rest and good food.'

'Guesthouse, then,' Frank assented cheerfully.

'Would you like me to make enquiries?'

'If it wouldn't be too much trouble.'

It was no trouble at all. Within a few days, she was back with news of a suitable place. She had found a retired garda sergeant and his wife, whose family had grown and scattered, leaving them with a large house and room to spare. They could offer him full board with a bedroom and sitting room on the ground floor for three pounds a week.

'It would be like having a flat of your own without the bother of preparing meals.'

'Just what the doctor ordered,' Frank said.

'Mrs Keane is a comfortable, homely person. I think you'll like her. The sergeant is easy-going. He likes fishing. Books too – they've a great lot of books.'

'Anyone who likes fishing and books is all right with me.'

It sounded a pleasant, civilised household to settle in until he had time to look around him and decide about the future. So, everything had been arranged.

'Will you come and visit me?' Frank asked tentatively.

'Are you just being polite, now, or do you mean that?' Sister Cooney looked at him closely.

'Of course I mean it. Otherwise I wouldn't ask.'

'Patients sometimes feel under an obligation,' she explained, 'and then, when the time comes, they regret it.'

'I'm not like that at all. You should know that.'

'Yes,' she said, 'I think I do.'

'You'll come, then?'

'I'd be delighted to.'

'I'll tell you what we'll do.' Frank took off his glasses and began to polish them in the sheet with enthusiasm. 'On your first evening off, we'll go out and have a meal – just a little celebration. How about that?'

'A little celebration would do you good,' Sister Cooney said, hiding her pleasure.

'Lazarus rising from the dead and all that!' Frank laughed.

Arty sat in sombre mood, thinking of death. Vincent had not turned up and he wondered what he could possibly say to him when – or if – he did. Death made little sense at the best of times. Death of the young made no sense at all. He sometimes wondered about his own death, but beyond thinking of himself on some long-distance collision course with annihilation, he could not imagine it. He had seen so many people die. At first it had been harrowing, but he had grown used to it. It was possible to view the death of others in a detached way, even – if one were honest – to take pleasure in it. There was the satisfaction of being a survivor, the morbid distinction of being first about with the news. It made eating and drinking a little more exciting to know

226

that someone else had just ceased doing these basic human things for ever.

He looked up as Phil strolled in, and the sight of him, standing there so ludicrously, so needlessly alive, made his mind veer like a weather vane in a high wind to a more frivolous way of thinking. Phil, with his soft, sprawling face, looked like an excrescence – an unhealthy toadstool, swelling with yeasty exuberance out of decayed wood.

'Hey, Phil,' he called, 'did you ever think of dying at all?'

Phil looked at him with bulging horror and searched around the metallic ward for some wood to touch, drumming his fingers at last in relief on the top of the locker. 'It's not right to be joking about things like that,' he said. He wondered if the effects of 'the electric' were wearing off and Byrne was going out of his mind again.

'It'll come one day and you'd be as well to be prepared.'

'I trusts in God,' Phil said. 'What more can I do?'

'Make your will. I'm going to make mine. Will you witness it for me?'

'It's not lucky to make a will. Don't you know that?'

'We'll make two,' Arty said, reaching for some writing paper. 'Tell you what, Phil, I'll leave all I have to you, if you leave me your entire estate.'

'What estate?'

'Your tenements and hereditaments, as the lawyers say, your pleasure gardens, your fishing rights and the family jewels.'

'Quit acting the cod, will you!' Phil said crossly.

'If that's the way you take it,' Arty said, 'I'll just have to leave it all to the ould fellow.'

'What have you to leave to anybody?' Phil sneered.

Arty whistled cheerfully as he pretended to write. 'Last will and testament of Arthur Byrne, deceased ...'

'It's not right, I tell you,' Phil said.

'To my revered father, whose massive intellect has been a formative influence from my tenderest years, I leave, will and bequeath ...'

'It's not natural for a son to be makin' fun of his father,' Phil protested.

'That's where you're wrong, Phil ould son!' Arty laid down his pen and geared himself up for argument. 'It's the most natural thing in the world. I read an article in *Reader's Digest* about this very clever fellow called Freud. Do you know what he said about fathers and sons?'

'Some daft fellow, I suppose,' Phil scoffed. 'How would I know what he said?'

'He said it was natural for every son to want to kill his father and marry his mother.'

Phil blessed himself quickly before speaking again. 'The dirty Communist!' he cried, his voice trembling with shock. 'That class o' talk is against the Catholic Church – against all the laws o' God and man. That book should be banned. People who say things like that should be locked up.'

'Freud was a genius,' Arty said, 'the cleverest man of his day.'

'He was a blackguard and no Catholic, whatever else he was!' Phil said. He stood up to indicate that the conversation was at an end and that he had no wish to be involved as a partner in such blasphemous and heretical talk.

When he had gone, Arty, smiling to himself at what he considered a victory, got out of bed and set off for the bathroom to wash his hair. He took with him a towel and a bag, tied at the neck with a drawstring, a bag that bulged with jars and bottles, containing shampoos and pomades and lotions. He whistled a tune as he strolled down the corridor. Baldness, he told himself – and smiled at his own joke – was a receding problem.

228

Madeleine seemed to like him as he was, so why should he worry about something that wasn't important any more?

It was spring outside. Sunlight lay on the grass. He stood at a window and looked down over the trees, where rooks were crossing sticks in a light sway of air. Like them, he was a survivor. It was possible to think of a future away from this place.

EPILOGUE

Green thickened the hedges again. Brown husks littered the paths under trees. High above, the wind played a delicate tune through crumpled foliage. Spring roared like fire through the grass. It was a year since he had come up this steep, winding avenue. He might have died – there was so little of his old self left.

He would be going out soon, but an umbilical cord would still tie him to this house of death. Once a fortnight, he would come up the avenue and round that last bend and – with a tightening in his bowels – see it there, becalmed in the grass. The spirits of Eileen and the Commander and of all who had died there, would crowd about him more densely than the blown petals of the flowering cherries. Their voices would cry in the falling sigh of wind around its gables.

An old Ford, with straight back and matchbox rear window, laboured up the avenue. He stood aside to let it pass. In the back seat a thin face stared ahead. It might have been himself a year ago. When he came within sight of the front door, the car was parked outside and two men were helping a third up the steps. The young man leaned heavily on them, his head sagging loosely. At the door Nurse Lambert stood waiting with a wheelchair – crisp, starched, bright as the April sunlight. She waved to him, before turning and wheeling her patient indoors.

The young man had seemed vaguely familiar. He wondered what his condition was and whether he would survive. Would he pull through and, like himself, fall in love – or imagine he was falling in love – with his nurse? He wondered if falling in love with the nurse wasn't a necessary stage of convalescence.

Out here in the open, with the world large around him and light beckoning from beyond the horizon, it was not easy to fit Keelan into whatever lay ahead for him. Inside it had been different. With the universe narrowed to the four walls and death abroad in the corridor, she was womankind – the other half of reality. Not to know her, not to love her (at the very least, not to want to love her) was to deny oneself the totality of experience. Could he still love her when she had ceased to be a symbol and walked in the lesser light of her own individuality? It was something that he would have to find out.

When he went upstairs, she was waiting for him. 'You look different in your clothes,' she said, 'almost like a stranger.'

'You'd look different out of uniform. You'd be almost a stranger too.'

'We'd both be strangers, then, if we met outside?'

'Maybe we would. I don't know.'

'You'll be away home in a short while.'

'I'll be back for refills.'

'They're always different when they come back,' Keelan said. 'Things look different from the outside.'

'I've been wondering about that,' he said.

'It's the way of the world,' she said with a wry smile.

There was something sad about the exchange – and a finality that he, by no means, approved of or desired. There was still the possibility that when they did meet outside, it would be a beginning, and not the end that neither wished for, but both half-expected.

'Time will tell,' he said.

'Whatever happens when you go out,' she said after a silence, 'you must mind your health. Don't be like poor Vincent. You saw him coming in, didn't you?'

'So, that's who it was!' he exclaimed. 'I thought he looked familiar.'

'Poor fellow!' she said. 'He's in a bad way.'

When she left him, he stood at the window for a long time, looking out over the newly-awakened countryside. Below him in the valley, the river slid by greening banks, the infinity of space mirrored on its smooth surface. He looked upwards. Clouds uncoiled from the south-west with unhurried grace. Above and beyond, the depths receded endlessly, mystery layered beyond mystery for ever.

Tuberculosis is a disease of the lungs and other organs, caught mainly by inhalation of the tubercle bacillus, which is present in the sputum of those who have already contracted the disease. The pulmonary form – which is highly contagious – attacks the lungs, but TB can also affect the bones, the spine, the joints, the glands and most internal organs. The commonest form manifests itself in coughing, spitting of infected sputum and blood, fever, night sweats, loss of weight – hence its medical name, phthisis, the wasting disease, or, in layman's language, consumption.

Until the discovery of drugs such as streptomycin and para-aminosalicylic acid, there was no effective cure for this disease, which claimed the lives of hundreds of young people in Ireland every year in the forties and fifties.